New Jersey Heat
David Huff

Book Four

David Huff Publishing
ISBN: 978-0-9988003-4-9
Library of Congress Control Number (Pending)
New Jersey Heat/ David Huff
Digital distribution | 2018.
Paperback | 2018

Dedication

This book is dedicated to all of my readers who have asked when is the next one coming out? May you enjoy this as well as the others.

"To know how to suggest is the great art of teaching. To attain it we must be able to guess what will interest... We must learn to read the childish soul as we might a piece of music. Then, by simply changing the key, we keep up the attraction and vary the song." — Henri-Frédéric Amiel, Journal Intime (Nov. 16, 1864)

"To know what you prefer instead of humbly saying Amen to what the world tells you, you ought to prefer, is to have kept your soul alive." — Robert Louis Stevenson

"To know and to act are one and the same." — Samurai maxim

"To know one thing, you must know the opposite just as much, else you don't know that one thing." — Henry Moore

"To know that one knows what one knows, and to know that one doesn't know what one doesn't know, there lies true wisdom." — Confucius

"To know that we know what we know, and that we do not know what we do not know, that is true knowledge." — Confucius

"To know what is right and not do it is the worst cowardice." — Confucius [Kung Fu-tse]

"To know all things is not permitted." — Horace

"To know that you do not know is the best. To pretend to know when you do not know is a disease." — Lao Tzu

Chapter I

As Miguel sat watching from the top of the mountain, he made himself comfortable in some buck brush. He lay in the shade, which was giving him protection from the sun and from prying eyes. His partner, Lucas Medina, a Border Patrol officer, was with him a hundred yards further down the same ridge line. Lucas was hiding behind some big boulders that rested on top of the ridge. Miguel was on loan to the Border Patrol, learning their way of tracking drug runners and illegals as they crossed the border into Arizona. From where they sat, with field glasses, they could see the valley below them for miles in any direction relative to the river, this river formed a natural boundary between Mexico and Arizona. In this small area in the corner of Arizona, the Colorado River was wide enough to need help crossing but not so deep you couldn't cross it. The mountain range that Lucas and Miguel were watching from was southwest of Yuma. This area was well known by the Border Patrol agents for trafficking of illegals trying to cross over into the United States.

Lucas called on the radio, "I see some movement on the west side of the river coming our way."

Miguel, using his glasses, spotted the movement after

scanning the area for a minute. He called back to Lucas, "I see it, looks like there's a group trying to cross over. You want to go down and check it out?"

"Not just yet, let's give them a little more time; besides, they haven't crossed the river yet."

"Roger that; I think you don't want to climb back up the mountain once you're down there," Miguel said, joking.

"Now, what would make you say that?" Lucas asked, laughing in the radio.

"Because I sure as hell don't want to climb back up myself; it was hard enough the first time."

At this time, they heard a popping sound coming from the valley below. As Miguel used his binoculars once again, he focused on the area where the movement was first spotted. From where he was he could see people running in all directions, some into the river and others running alongside the river. By now, Lucas was watching what was happening below and called out on the radio, "Holy crap; those people down there are being shot at!"

Both Miguel and Lucas were making their way down the mountain to get close enough to see better and to stop the shooting. Getting closer to the river, they found a group of rocks they could hide behind. As they crouched there they could hear the people screaming as they were trying to get away. The two men who were firing at the people were laughing at the ones who were wounded and continued shooting their guns at them to finish them off. Miguel, from his position, spotted one of the shooters and was close enough with his rifle to fire, and as he did so he dropped one of the gunmen. The second gunman, seeing that his partner was down, started looking around, trying to find the other shooter. Having no luck, he fired in the direction of where he thought the shot had come from. Miguel took aim and fired again, this time wounding the second shooter. As Lucas and Miguel got up from their positions, they moved closer to the scene. They both could see people lying on the ground; some of them were dead and others were wounded. Lucas, calling on the radio, asked for assistance to help with the bodies and to get medical attention for the wounded. Miguel walked over to the second gunman and looked at him lying on the desert floor. He could tell that he would live and stand trial for the murders of his fellow countrymen. Lucas was busy assisting with the wounded, trying to help those that were badly hurt by doing all he could to stop the bleeding. As they waited for medical help to arrive, they kept an eye out for any other survivors, knowing most of them would rather hide until dark and then continue their trek into the U.S. When the medical help came, the EMTs got busy working on the wounded and prepping them for the ride to the nearest hospital. Pretty soon the Mexican military showed up in their two-and-a-half-ton trucks, pulling up to where the shooting had taken place. A captain from the first truck came over and looking over the situation, introduced himself to Miguel and Lucas, "My name is Diego Montoya, I am the commanding officer of this area and we will take over from here."

Miguel and Lucas stared at him for a moment.

"I'm sorry, Captain, they are on U.S. soil now; they fall under our jurisdiction," Lucas said.

The captain pulled out a paper from his pocket to show them. "No matter, they come back with us."

After looking at the paper, Miguel asked Lucas, "What does it say?"

"As per agreement between our country and their country, we need to let these people go back with them."

"Some of these people are shot up pretty bad. If you take them, there's a chance some of them won't make it," Miguel said angrily.

"Senor, that is not your problem; it is mine to worry about."

The captain motioned for the sergeant to get the soldiers started loading the bodies onto one of the trucks. The wounded were haphazardly loaded next onto the other truck. Lucas, watching all of this, started yelling and threatening the soldiers not to touch the wounded.

Miguel went over and grabbed him, "Look around you."

By now, Lucas saw what Miguel was talking about. He could see that all the military soldiers in the trucks had their rifles trained on him and were waiting for the word to shoot him. The captain yelled at his men to put their weapons down and then walked over to where Miguel and Lucas were standing.

"Do you really want to create an international incident over these poor people?" the captain said, smiling.

Lucas, shaking his head, replied, "No, I don't think so."

"Besides, they are nobody to you or to anybody else. Good day, gentlemen; rest assured, we will take care of them ourselves."

Miguel, Lucas, and the medical staff stood there watching as the captain and his men continued loading the wounded and the dead on to the trucks. All they could do was stand there and feel helpless, knowing that these people would all be dead soon.

Chapter II

Later that evening, Miguel and Lucas drove back to the Border Patrol station and reported to the station captain what had happened to the illegals after crossing to the American side of the border.

After listening, the captain shook his head. "I know you don't agree with the Mexican army captain. But according to the Memorandum of Agreement (MOA), we have no other recourse but to let the people go back to their country."

"You know, some of those people that went back are going to die because of this MOA, don't you?" asked Miguel.

"Do you think I agree with this MOA? Well, I don't, and that being said, it's above my pay grade to change it and I'm not losing my job over it," the captain snapped back at Miguel.

"So how do we do our jobs now?" asked Lucas.

"You monitor the border, confiscate the drugs, and send the people back across the border. That's all you do, or at least until we get new directions to follow," replied the captain.

Miguel looked at Lucas. "No need for me to stay here any longer. I'll be heading back to Phoenix tomorrow."

"I wish I was going with you."

"Me too."

The next morning, Miguel loaded his suitcase into the trunk of his car and after saying goodbye to Lucas, he started his drive back to Phoenix. It was only a three-hour drive from the border to Phoenix, and after being gone for a week he was anxious to get home to Marissa and the kids. The drive back was uneventful. After arriving home in the afternoon, the kids and Marissa met him at the door, giving Miguel hugs and kisses.

Miguel looked at each one of his kids and hugged each of them. "Have you guys grown at least a foot since I left?"

The kids laughed at their dad. "You're being silly, Daddy," and they ran away laughing.

Marissa looked on as he chased the kids around the house, finally catching Peter, then Sarah, and then Jennifer. As he held them he started tickling them, which sent them into hyper drive, running all around the house.

"All right, you kids; you need to let Daddy rest a while to catch his breath."

All of the kids started saying, "But Daddy's home to play with us, and we never get to play with Daddy anymore."

Marissa was putting her foot down on the kids' complaints so that she didn't have to fight them for his attention. "Mommy hasn't seen daddy, either. I need some time with him. Look, it's time for your favorite show."

With that, the kids headed into the next room to turn on the TV and start watching "The Story Pig."

"Thank goodness for 'The Story Pig,'" Miguel said.

"You don't know the half of it!" Marissa said as she came over and kissed Miguel. "It's the only time I get a break from the kids nowadays."

"So how was it working with the Border Patrol?" Marissa asked as they sat on the couch talking.

"It wasn't too bad, but they have some strange rules they have to follow when it comes to catching the illegals. They have to let them go, even if they're on our side of the border," Miguel said, disapprovingly.

"That doesn't make any sense at all," Marissa said, surprised at his statement.

"The one thing that was different in this case was there were no drugs being carried by any of them. The guides that were helping them to get into the U.S. were also the ones trying to kill them."

"I wonder why that was the case?"

"I wonder if it had to do with the Mexican National Army being nearby?" Miguel said, questioning the timing of the army appearing out of nowhere.

By now, it was time for dinner. As the kids helped set the table, Miguel took a shower to get the daily grime off of him. When he showed up at the dinner table, the kids were already seated and waiting for their dad to start eating. After dinner Miguel helped Marissa with the dishes, rinsing them and putting them in the dishwasher. It was his way of helping while she got the kids ready for bed. When it was time, he would read the kids a bedtime story after they were settled in each of their beds. The children always looked forward to Daddy reading those stories at night. Usually it was a book with animals and Miguel would make the animals' noises to make the stories more exciting. It always took Marissa a little longer to settle them down because of Miguel's storytelling. She didn't mind so much because he was being a good father to the kids and making up for lost time for being gone.

When the kids were all tucked in bed and asleep, that was the quiet time Miguel and Marissa enjoyed the most. Then Miguel would watch TV with Marissa until Marissa fell asleep on his shoulder or cuddled up next to him. By nine o'clock both of them were ready to go to bed.

On his first day back at work in the narcotics unit, Miguel reported to the chief to let him know he was back and ready to go to work.

Chad looked at Miguel. "The police chief needs to see you right away."

"Do you know what it's about?"

"He didn't say anything to me about it. Now get going; they're expecting you up there in the ivory tower."

The term "ivory tower" was used to imply the part of the building where the high-ranking decision makers worked. You didn't get called there unless a good thing or a really bad thing had happened.

Miguel made his way to the ivory tower to meet the police chief. Stopping at the secretary's desk, he let her know who he was. The secretary looked at Miguel, "Take a seat, I'll let him know you are here."

The secretary knocked on the police chief's door and went in. A few seconds later she reappeared at the door. "The police chief will see you now."

Miguel walked into the chief's office and stood there for a moment while the he finished a phone call. Hanging up the phone, the chief stood up and smiled as he moved around the desk and offered his hand to Miguel. The chief motioned for him to sit in one of the leather chairs in the center of the room. Miguel, after shaking the chief's hand, sat down and waited to hear what he had to say.

As Miguel sat there a moment, the secretary came in again with some paperwork in her hand. Giving it to the chief he looked it over. As Miguel sat there watching, he began wondering what this was all about. Finally, the chief raised his eyes towards Miguel. "How long have you been on the force now?"

"About ten years, sir."

"Do you like what you're doing here on the force?"

"Yes, I enjoy it very much, sir," Miguel said,

wondering about the questions coming from the chief. "Am I getting fired, sir?"

The chief laughed. "No, you're not; in fact, not at all. This is a letter of appreciation. It comes from the Border Patrol, where you were assigned as a liaison this last week. According to the letter, you kept a Border Patrol agent from getting shot and prevented an international incident from occurring."

Miguel was stunned at the letter from the Border Patrol. "I didn't do anything, sir; I just did what anybody else would've done," said Miguel humbly.

"Well, you did the right thing at the right time for all involved. And you made us look good here in Phoenix by your actions."

"Thank you; I don't know what to say, sir."

"Well, I do. Your cool thinking saved people's lives out there, and no one got hurt because of it," said the chief, almost busting his buttons. "And because of it, you're promoted to lieutenant. Your test results came back and you passed the exam."

Miguel was shocked at the good news and didn't know what to say, except, "Thank you."

The secretary opened the door and let Miguel's boss in, along with his team-mates, to congratulate him on his promotion. Miguel, still feeling overwhelmed at all of this, just stood there with a big grin on his face as everybody shook his hand and patted him on the back. After five minutes of shaking hands and saying congratulations to him, Miguel's boss kicked his teammates out of the chief's office. The chief asked him to sit down again, as well as Miguel's boss, in the leather chairs.

"Now that you are promoted, you'll need to find another place to work," the chief said.

"I think he needs to be someplace where he can't hurt anybody," Chad said, smiling.

"I agree, maybe a new unit that hasn't been created yet, maybe a new unit working with the other state and federal agencies around here," said the chief, smiling.

"I don't know, being a liaison with the others could be too much for him. What do you think about this, Miguel?" Chad asked.

"I think I could learn to like it, sir," Miguel said, smiling.

With that, everybody laughed, and the chief said, "Then it's official. You will be working in the federal building alongside the FBI and the other agencies inside the Department of Justice."

"Thank you, sir," Miguel said as he shook both of their hands.

Chad looked at him for a second. "Get your gear out of my office, stat."

Miguel left the chief's office and made his way back to the narcotics unit and started picking up his stuff from off the desk that had been his for the last four years. One of his teammates already had a box sitting on the desk when he got there to load his stuff. In about 30 minutes he had all his belongings in the box and was on his way to the federal building, looking for a person by the name of Special Agent Smith. When Miguel arrived at the federal building, he asked security, "What floor is the FBI office on?"

"Second floor, first door on the right," replied the security officer.

Taking the elevator to the second floor and opening the first door on the right, Miguel walked in and saw Lucas sitting there in one of the chairs with his head leaning back against the wall.

Miguel kicked Lucas's chair, "Somebody ought to call security right now."

Lucas, surprised by the kick, stood up; and it took a second for Lucas to recognize Miguel before wrapping his arms around him, almost causing Miguel to drop the box of stuff he was carrying.

"So what brings you here?" asked Lucas.

"I made somebody mad saving your life and now I'm being sent here to work out my time before I go to my real job."

"You too, as well? They said I was too dangerous out there working the border, so they sent me here for rehab."

"Where do I find this Special Agent Smith?"

"I don't know, except they told me to sit here and wait for him."

"Well, we can wait together, I guess."

After waiting another five minutes Special Agent Smith came walking through the door and, looking at the two sitting there, "I take it you guys know each other?" Both Miguel and Lucas nodded their heads in unison, standing up. "Well, follow me and I'll show you where you can park yourselves and your gear."

With that, they followed Agent Smith to another set of doors and pushing through, he pointed to the two empty desks next to his. "These two desks are yours. Make yourselves comfortable; I'll be back in ten minutes."

Miguel looked at Lucas. "Which desk do you want?"

"I'll take that desk over there, which is closest to the window."

Miguel looked at him, smiling, knowing there were no windows in the room. "All right, you take the desk closest to Smith's desk. That way, if he gets mad, he'll hit you first and that will give me time to get out of the office."

"Fair enough; this way I can be teacher's pet."

After getting their desks squared away, Agent Smith came in with a stack of cases to be looked at by the team. Miguel asked, "What are we going to be working on?"

"We're going to be working on human trafficking, as well as drug trafficking and anything else that comes across the border," Smith said.

"What shall we call you?" asked Lucas.

"You can call me Smith or Agent Smith, but never call me Mr. Smith," he said, smiling. "I need you two to read these cases and decide between yourselves which ones you want to do first. Oh, by the way, the coffee pot is in the outer room in the corner. I suggest you guys make yourselves comfortable and grab a cup of coffee before you start."

The two looked at each other and smiled, "So, when does the fun start?" Miguel asked sarcastically.

"I think my fun meter is already pegged," Lucas said, sounding like he had lost the war.

After a couple of hours of going through the cases, the two men had a pile showing the ones they were interested in versus the other pile that they considered not a priority. By the third hour they were discussing the last two cases together.

After lunch was completed, they decided to work on the Palmer case, which dealt with human trafficking from Mexico to the United States. The case involved the drug cartels offering their services to the South American and Mexican immigrants wanting to cross into the United States illegally. The scenario was the same for much of the other cases. The immigrants would make their way to Mexico by paying for their own trip. Then the cartels would have the immigrants stay at a town close to the U.S. border and pay 4,500 dollars each, more in some cases, plus some sort of tax to the criminal organization that was helping them get to America. If they couldn't pay the price, the cartels would offer them the chance to go as mules, hauling drugs across the border. This, in most cases, would end up with the mules being killed by the coyotes (cartel guides) after the drugs were delivered. For the immigrants, there'd be no guarantee that doing it this way would get them to America. As always, the risk was placed solely on the immigrants.

By the time they chose the Palmer case, Agent Smith was back at his desk, waiting to hear from Miguel and Lucas about the case they had decided on.

"Well, what case did you decide to work on?" asked Smith.

"We decided to work on the Palmer case, because, first of all, it's more current than the rest and poses the greatest threat to the immigrants coming to America," Miguel said.

"Oh, you did, did you?" replied Smith.

"We figure this one would really be a challenge for us, with the biggest impact on the trafficking issue," Lucas added.

"Very well, what do we do first?" asked Smith.

"We establish a contact that we can trust in the town of Nogales, which is in the southern Mexican state of Sonora, a stone's throw from the Arizona border. We need to get into the group and learn of their routes and the coyotes they use," said Miguel.

"How do we do that?" asked Smith.

"We go undercover and work our way back to the United States via the cartel," said Lucas.

"Now you know why you were chosen for this assignment. Both of you are not your typical American citizens; that is, you're not white and you, especially you, Miguel, come from a South American country. Lucas here is from old Mexico, at least his family is, and will be able to pass himself off as a Mexican migrant," Smith added, "You were chosen because you know how to adapt to your surroundings and survive. We need you to go undercover and find out how the cartel gets the immigrants across the border."

"What do you mean we're not white?" Lucas said, smiling.

Smith looked at him and chuckled. "I know it's hard to believe, but if you look in the mirror you'll see what I mean." He continued, "You guys are here to find out about the captain you had a run-in with on the border and the men behind the killing of the immigrants trying to cross the border."

Miguel and Lucas got somber thinking about what had happened in the valley a couple of weeks ago. The memories were still fresh in their minds.

"The problem is that the captain and his men might recognize you from the encounter you had with him," Smith said. "I want you two to consider what you're getting yourselves into before we start. If you choose not to do this one, we can choose another case to work."

"In Colombia, where I am from, there were plenty of people like the captain and his men. They were opportunists looking to make money, no matter the cost to human life…" Miguel stopped and started thinking of his boyhood in Colombia, and for a moment was quiet. Then, collecting his thoughts, he said, "I'll do it."

Lucas thought about the people they had to leave behind with the captain and his men. "I want the captain to pay for what he did out there in the desert that day."

"I'm glad to hear it. Now the real fun begins," said Smith. "I'll be your handler, for the lack of better words. I will pose as a tourist looking for a good time in Nogales and meet you there on an irregular basis."

"How will we get in touch with you?" asked Miguel.

"There is an Appleby's in Nogales; I will be there every two weeks from seven o'clock pm till nine o'clock on Sunday nights, eating, and we will meet there. Does that work for you guys?" asked Smith.

"Hopefully, it shouldn't be a problem; however, what if we can't make the meeting for some unknown reason?" asked Miguel.

"We'll put tracker tags on each of you guys before you go out into the field. Our satellites in the sky will know where you are at all times. If you can't keep the meeting time, I'll have your trackers to tell me where you are and, if necessary, we'll come and get you," Smith said.

After the meeting Smith had them go to the medical office in the next hallway and have the trackers implanted in their shoulders. After they were finished in the medical office they headed back to their desks. Now the only thing left to decide was when and where they would enter into Mexico and start their adventure to bring down the cartel and their human trafficking operation.

When Miguel got home, he told Marissa about the job promotion and moving over to the FBI office to work with the Border Patrol and the FBI. "This is going to be a special task force to break up the human trafficking operation and maybe stop the drug flow into the United States, as well."

Marissa was concerned about the part of Miguel going undercover in Mexico. "How will I know you'll be all right while you're gone?" she asked with tears in her eyes.

"I'll have Special Agent Smith contact you once a week on Sunday night to let you know I'm doing fine," Miguel said as he held Marissa. "Somebody has to be able to stop this human trafficking and drug running. I've seen what it does to my people in Colombia; it is not good," Miguel angrily said.

"I know you must do this. I don't want to lose you as my husband and father to our kids," Marissa said, crying as she hugged him.

"It'll be all right. If we run into trouble, call my

parents and they'll come and help you anytime and anyplace. Promise me you'll do this?"

"I promise; I'll call them at the earliest possible time if I know you're in trouble."

With that, they sat on the couch and just held each other without saying a word.

Chapter III

Miguel left for work earlier than usual this morning, calling a cab to come and get him. Arriving at the federal building, he met with Lucas and Smith, all of them dressed down for their part in the operation. Smith had a car waiting to take them to a known hangout for illegals.

"There is someone I want you to meet," Smith said as he drove.

Smith parked the car and the three of them walked into a small building adjacent to a food kitchen. He introduced them to the lady who ran the soup kitchen.

Smith, shaking hands with the lady, said, "This is Amanda. She is a miracle worker in helping these people have a place to sleep and food to eat, all without help from the city," he added. "The money she needs to run this place comes from the sales of her artwork and sculpturing."

She brushed her hair back from her face and reached out to shake their hands, as well.

"What can I do for you this morning?" she cheerfully asked.

"These are the two I was telling you about yesterday,"

Smith said.

"Oh yes, I remember now; a lot has happened since yesterday."

"We need your help in getting across the border and getting to the right people in Mexico," Smith said.

Looking around, she called Fernando to come over, speaking fluent Spanish, said, "These two men need to get over into Mexico and meet with the people you know they can trust, in order to find the captain and his men and bring them to justice."

Fernando shook his head in agreement. "One of my brothers was killed by this captain and his men. I will help you to get him and his boss, if possible."

Lucas stood looking at Amanda and noticed that she was a wisp of a woman, standing a little over five-and-a-half feet tall, weighing maybe a hundred pounds soaking wet; her hair was cut like a tomboy's, yet she still looked like a lady. She seemed pretty sure of herself in all that she was doing. She had clear blue eyes that, when looking at her, you could tell she was on a mission. Lucas fell in love with her at first sight and couldn't help but stare at her. As for Amanda, if she saw it, she didn't let on. Amanda was busy with her job of getting breakfast ready for the homeless that were already there. Lucas didn't say anything but started helping Amanda with her tasks, setting up the food trays, utensils and plates. Miguel couldn't help but notice this and elbowed Smith, nodding in the direction of Lucas, as he watched what was happening. Amanda was smiling at Lucas as he joked with her, and she would occasionally brush her hair out of the way as she talked with Lucas.

Smith looked at Miguel, "I think Lucas is twitterpated with Amanda, what do you think?"

"I think he is in love and is hooked really bad," Miguel said, smiling.

After breakfast all three of the men went with Fernando to the border and crossed over, with Smith staying on the American side. After all of them shook hands and said good luck, Miguel and Lucas disappeared into the old city of Nogales, following Fernando to find the captain. Smith watched until he couldn't see them anymore, all the while praying that these two would return safely back to him. For being a stone-cold man in some ways and having only known them for a short time, Smith worried about Miguel and Lucas like a father worries about his children when they're gone for the first time. The success of this operation and the others to follow would depend on Miguel and Lucas coming home safe and sound. As Smith turned away, he headed back to his car and sat for a moment, thinking about if he had missed anything as far as the safety of Miguel and Lucas. With nothing coming to mind, he headed back to the federal building in Phoenix.

Miguel and Lucas followed Fernando into the city,

staying on the main streets, following the people as they made their way to run their errands. Lucas and Miguel couldn't believe how trashy and dirty the city was in comparison to its counterpart in America. For Miguel, it was like coming home to Colombia and being on the bad side of Bogota. Lucas was amazed at the people and how they lived here. The Mexican people were dressed in shirts and pants that were old and worn out. These types of clothes on the American side, especially the Levi's the kids wore, would sell for an extra hundred dollars apiece. After reaching the city center, Fernando took them into a bar and told them to take a seat in the corner. Being dark and cool, it took a minute to acclimate to their surroundings. Sitting in the dark corner gave Miguel and Lucas a good view of the front door. From there they could see Fernando over at the bar, talking to the bartender. In about five minutes Fernando came over and sat down at the table with Miguel and Lucas.

"The cartel people are looking for two Americans traveling through Nogales as migrant workers," Fernando said.

Miguel looked at Fernando, "Are they looking for us?"

"I'm not sure as of yet, but we will wait till darkness falls to leave here," said Fernando.

"Are we safe here?" asked Lucas, rather anxious.

"We are safe here until tonight, and then we must

leave," Fernando said.

Miguel and Lucas stayed put for the next three hours in the bar killing time nursing their beers, all the while trying to figure out how the cartel people found out about them coming into Nogales. In the meantime, Fernando went out into the street to find out what was known about the two gringos coming over.

Fernando came back. "It's time to go; we must leave now. The cartel people are patrolling the streets."

Miguel and Lucas followed Fernando out of the bar through the back door and waited in the shadows of the alleyway, watching for anybody that didn't look like they belonged there. Fernando went first, leading the way across the street. Miguel and Lucas were watching from the alley when a small truck came around the corner and had Fernando in its headlights. Fernando froze in place and waited for the truck to stop. As it stopped, two men got out of the truck with guns and started asking Fernando questions. Miguel and Lucas had their semi-autos out and pointed at the two gunmen talking to Fernando.

One of the gunmen asked Fernando, "Why are you out so late by yourself?"

Fernando, pointing at the cantina, replied, "I was drinking in the cantina and forgot what time it was."

The second gunman looked at Fernando. "Where do you live?"

Fernando didn't answer at first but pointed down the

street over in the direction of the center of town. The second gunman hit him, and Fernando went down, landing on his hands and knees. The second gunman kicked him in the ribs, which knocked Fernando face down on the ground. The first gunman slid the loading mechanism on his AK-47 back and loaded a round into the chamber.

By now, Fernando was saying, "I live on Montoya Street near the market."

The first gunman thought for a moment. "There is no Montoya street; you lie to us."

He then pointed his gun at Fernando, ready to shoot him, at which time Miguel and Lucas fired their weapons, and both gunmen fell to the ground dead. Fernando got up and grabbed their weapons. Miguel and Lucas came out of the alley to help Fernando.

"Help me load the bodies into the back of the truck," Fernando said.

Miguel and Lucas did as they were told. Miguel hopped into the back of truck with the bodies and Fernando and Lucas got into the cab of the truck and drove out of Nogales to the outskirts of town. Ditching the bodies of the gunmen there, they stayed with the truck until they were in Santa Anna. When they arrived there, Fernando stopped at the first gas station to put more fuel in the truck and get some food for the trip.

"We make good time this way, but once they find the bodies they will be looking for us, especially this truck," he said, looking at Miguel and Lucas.

"How much further is it to where we are going?" asked Lucas.

"We are headed to a place I know of in Hermosillo. We can get rid of the truck there and we can walk from there to where we need to go."

Once the truck was refueled and the food was bought, they got back into the truck and headed south on Highway 15 to Hermosillo. The trip to the city took only ninety minutes. Being only 167 miles from the U.S. border, 'The City in the Sun', Hermosillo, is the capital of the state of Sonora. It is also close to Sinaloa. Having to stop once at the checkpoint going into Hermosillo, Fernando did all the talking, claiming that he was only carrying two Americans looking for a good time in Hermosillo, no questions were asked, and they were able to continue on their drive.

Once arriving in Hermosillo, Fernando took Miguel and Lucas to a home in the northeast part of the city along Boulevard Morelos. Here Miguel and Lucas wouldn't attract attention if they were seen by any of the locals. Miguel could tell the area was building up as a nice area to move to with dining and shopping available for the locals, hoping more of the Americans and Canadians would be stopping to stay here. Lucas was impressed with how modern the city was, noticing they had a Wal-Mart as well. After walking around a little, Miguel looked at Lucas. "I wouldn't mind being assigned to work here as part of the Border Patrol for the U.S."

Miguel agreed with Lucas's feelings, as well. The city was a beautiful place. The locals were friendly and, for the most part, everybody spoke English. It was cleaner than some of the border towns Lucas had worked in for the past five years. They both wondered why there was such a contrast between Hermosillo, being so clean and modern, versus Nogales, in old Mexico, being dirty and trashy.

Farther down the highway was Sinaloa, a known area for drugs and the cartel. Both of them knew it would be the next stop on their way to see and learn about human trafficking and maybe drug trafficking, as well. Miguel and Lucas stayed with Fernando's family for the next couple of days while Fernando did some checking on the goings-on in Sinaloa. Fernando knew that the drug and human trafficking went through Hermosillo because highway 15 led straight to Nogales.

However, because of beefed-up security near Nogales, the cartel now went across the desert, where any wall or fence was nonexistent, and the border could be crossed by driving through. There were a couple of ranches that paralleled the border between Mexico and the United States. Most of the terrain was so rough that it was ideal for drug running and human trafficking. The Border Patrol can't see what's hidden in some of the valleys, not only because of the terrain, but also because of the camouflage the cartel uses to cover up their tracks and garbage.

The desert on the Mexican side of the border was used as a staging area into America. The coyotes knew when the Border Patrol was watching that area. In that case, they would take another trail or wait until the Border Patrol was out of sight. With people helping on the American side, i.e., bringing food and water to the border for the people, the cartel could stay out in the desert for days, waiting for the right time to cross into the United States. The worst part of the open-fenced area was finding the bodies of the ones that didn't make it or were killed by the cartel people who brought them there.

The cartel had taken over the business of human and drug trafficking and had teams set up on both sides of the border, making sure the drugs and people got into the United States. Any opposition by the ranch owners means that the ranchers could be the next bodies found out in the desert. The cartel has made it damn near impossible to stem the tide of people and drugs coming into the U.S. There is so much desert to watch and not enough personnel from the Border Patrol or any other law-enforcement agency to watch all of it. This is where the real war was being fought in the battle against the cartels in the southwestern United States and Mexico.

After two days, and leaving the truck behind, Miguel and Lucas headed down to Sinaloa, with Fernando again leading the way. Fernando knew that this area was always being watched by the cartel. Trying to avoid the watchers was going to be the hard part of the trip. Walking across the desert was the only way to move into the territory of the cartel safely. Leaving in the early part of the night, they made their way across the desert to find the trail that would lead them to the cartel headquarters in Sinaloa. Most of the trafficking done by the cartel was done using vehicles until they reached the border. All roads to and from Hermosillo were being watched by the cartel soldiers; therefore, Fernando was hoping to get through undetected by walking the distance. This would require them to walk at night and find a place to hole up during the day, hiding in the brush or mesquite trees to avoid detection by the cartel soldiers and others traveling through the area. This way they could get in and out of the cartel compounds without ever being seen.

By the second day, walking at night had taken its toll on everybody. The trail was bad during the day but worse at night. Without being able to see clearly, they ended up tripping on the rocks and roots of the plants, which created its own problems of trying not to sprain an ankle or break a leg. Realizing that traveling at night wasn't feasible anymore, they sat together to discuss all their options.

"How about we travel in the early morning instead of at night? That way we can see the trail as the sun rises,"

Lucas suggested to Fernando.

"It may take longer to get to the cartel compound if we do as you suggest," Fernando replied.

Both men were looking at Miguel at this point to break the deadlock between them.

"I think we can spare a couple of days to get there safely," Miguel said.

In the end, moving in the early morning light made it so that they were able to move quicker and with fewer problems from Mother Nature. Twice, when they were moving, they had to stop and hide from the gunmen looking for anybody lost in the desert. Miguel and Lucas let the gunmen go by just so they wouldn't attract attention or put light on their whereabouts. This would pay off in the long run for them, although they didn't realize it at the time. It took them three more days to get to Sinaloa and another day to move around to find the cartel's compound.

On the third day all three of the men sat on the edge of a ridge, looking down into the compound at the house where the boss of the cartel operated from. From what they could see there was one road in and out of the five-acre parcel of land. The compound had a cinderblock wall around it with concertina wire across the top of it. There were two guards at the front of the compound gate. Their job was to check the vehicles entering and leaving the compound. There were guards walking around inside the compound with AK-

47s and handguns for interior security. Lucas counted five guards walking around inside the compound, along with the two guards at the gate and possibly more inside the second building which looked like a bunk house for the men. On the outside of the compound there was a big wide-open space devoid of any vegetation, which stretched out about 100 yards from the base of the wall. This would be considered a killing zone for anybody trying to attack the compound. All three of the men assumed that the killing zone was either lined with sensors or mines or probably both. There were floodlights on the corners of the wall for looking in and looking out into the open ground on both sides of the compound. Using binoculars, Miguel could see cameras hanging in the corners of the house, which meant that there was a security team inside the house watching the videos from the cameras 24/7. There was a helicopter sitting in the open field next to the house.

After two days of watching the compound Miguel and Lucas realized that the only traffic coming and going were the trucks bringing in food and local girls for the guards for when they were off duty. The girls would stay overnight and leave the next morning in the same trucks that brought them in. The boss rarely left the compound, except when he needed to go to Mexico City or Hermosillo. Fernando knew this from his experience of seeing the helicopter flying to Hermosillo when he lived there. As the three men sat there in the shade of the mesquite trees, they started to think of ways to get into the compound to get the computer with all the trafficking information on it to take back with them.

The closest town to the cartel base was Culiacan, this town was owned and run by the cartel; it's about 900 miles from the U.S. border. The supplies that were needed for the cartel came from this town, including the girls. In the town the gunmen would ride in their trucks with the windows shaded so the passersby couldn't see inside the vehicles. There were men standing on the corners in town watching everything going on and basically keeping an eye on everybody who lived there. The gunmen would travel in groups throughout the town, shooting whomever they wanted, to ensure that fear was in place for what these men would do and to deter anybody from trying to take over the city. Anybody making a move to leave the town without permission was either shot on sight or never seen again. The rule of law was that nothing happened without the cartel boss knowing about it. The amount of money was always paid up front, before anybody left the city. If you couldn't pay, you either stayed or you worked as a mule to pay your way to America. If you were female, depending on your age and looks, you would have to sell your body or be a mule or both to leave the town. And becoming a mule or selling your body didn't guarantee that you would make it to America. You could be shot just short of the border, or, depending on the mood of the guards, they may let you cross over after they raped you and stole all your belongings. For the immigrants, looking for a better way to live always included going through hell first, if the guards even decided to let you live.

By now, Miguel and Lucas were ready to go into town to get something to eat and clean up from being in the desert for over two weeks. They kept in touch with Smith via the satphone and Marissa would be called by Smith to let her know everything was okay with Miguel. Fernando was ready to go into town, as well; living off the land wasn't all it was cracked up to be. Again, with Fernando leading the way into Culiacan, they left at night to keep a low profile in the city. Entering the city on the south end of town, where the locals lived, they moved in the shadows, making sure they were not being followed by anyone. Even the locals couldn't be trusted because the fear of retribution for aiding anybody would be hard on the men and their families. The Zona Centro had some hotels to sleep in and restaurants to choose from for food and drink. Having walked in instead of flying into Culiacan was the safest way of getting into the city. After getting a room and taking showers, putting on some clean clothes they had bought, the three men were ready to eat some hot food. Finding a restaurant, they settled into their chairs, looking at the menus to choose what they would have for dinner. After dinner they headed back to the motel. While watching some TV, Miguel had an idea come to him on how to get in the compound.

"Why don't we become the truck drivers going to and from the compound?" said Miguel.

"That's a good idea; the only problem is how do we become the drivers and not arouse any suspicion?" asked Lucas.

"We find out where they buy their food and pick up the girls and we hijack the drivers," Miguel said, feeling pretty good about coming up with the idea. "Maybe they make a stop before going into the compound and we get rid of the drivers and, wearing their outer clothes, we drive in with the supplies and drive out with the computer."

Fernando, who had been listening the whole time, said, "It won't be easy finding their stops along the way or where they go for food. I don't have any connections in this town that I know of."

Miguel thought about this for a moment. "We just need to find out where the girls come from and follow the trail from there." Miguel continued, "All we need to do is find the place where they go to pick up the girls and maybe dress up as one of the girls and get in the back of the truck."

Lucas smiled. "I don't think it'll work, simply because

I didn't shave my legs."

They all laughed at the comment and all concluded it would be safer to hijack the drivers and go from there, getting into the compound.

The next few days were spent on sightseeing, looking for the places the trucks would go to get their supplies for the compound. In fact, while they were walking around, Lucas pointed out to the other two the cartel helicopter flying overhead going in the direction of Hermosillo. After a while, Fernando took off on his own, looking for the grocery store that sold the food in bulk. Miguel and Lucas, acting like tourists, were taking in all the sights and visiting the local cantinas in the area. Seated in the back area of the cantinas, they watched and listened, waiting for some piece of information to slip out from the locals as they sat and drank at the bar.

As the days continued, the deeper they went into the parts of town that were not known by the tourists, where only the locals would go. Slipping into the Star-Bright cantina and sitting in the corner, Lucas and Miguel were hardly indistinguishable from the locals already in the bar. They watched the barmaids serve drinks to the customers while trying to pick up men at the different tables as they sat there drinking. Miguel pointed out to Lucas one of the men at the bar had a gun in his waistband. As he continued scanning the rest of the room, he noticed one of the girls was trying to get the attention of a man who was talking to his friend at the bar. They could see that the man at the bar was getting annoyed. Finally, he got mad at the girl and hit her, yelling, "Get away from me, you ugly cow!" He then started laughing with the man he was talking to.

The girl picked herself up from the floor and stood there a moment with blood trailing down her lip. She continued with the other men in the bar. As she made her way to where Miguel and Lucas were sitting, she tried to get Miguel to buy her a drink. Miguel agreed, "What do you like to drink?"

Seeing as how Miguel took her up on the drink, the girl sat down at their table and motioned to the bartender to bring her favorite drink. One of the other girls brought the drink over to the table and left them alone with the girl.

"Who's the man that hit you?" Miguel asked.

"Oh, he's one of the men that work for the cartel."

"What is your name?" Lucas asked.

"My name is Maria."

"Are you from around here?" Lucas continued questioning her.

"No, I am from Hermosillo and I work here for the money to go back home someday."

"The man who hit you, what does he do?" asked Miguel.

"Oh, he is one of the big guys for the cartel. He comes here a couple of times a week to talk to the man you see him with." She continued, "He is one of the big guys who is in charge of the men who work at the place in the building up on the hill."

"Do you know him very well?" asked Lucas.

"His name is Ricardo; he is a bad man and he likes to hurt the girls when he comes in here," she said, sneering.

"Does he usually come in alone when he comes here?" Miguel asked.

"Yes, he is dropped off by his friends and is picked up in an hour or two after he is drunk." Maria, looking at Lucas for the first time, continued, "Why do you ask so many questions about him?"

"I do not like men who hit ladies just for fun," Lucas said sarcastically.

She nodded in agreement. "Nobody likes him. All the girls are afraid of him, especially when his friends come in with him; they are mean to the girls all the time."

"Do you know where he lives?" asked Miguel.

"He lives in the house up in the mountains where the cartel is."

When the conversation ran out as did her drink, Maria got up from the table and went back to finding other men to buy her a drink. Miguel looked at her and after a bit of time asked Lucas, "So how do we handle this one?"

"We could follow him, but without a car we'd be out

of luck being able to track him anywhere."

"How about we wait for him outside and watch where he goes from here?"

"Good idea."

Both men got up, walked outside and waited in the shadows of the alley. When Ricardo walked outside, he paused a while, breathing in the night air. Lighting a cigarette, he stood there for a moment, then headed down the street toward the hotel. Miguel and Lucas, watching, followed in the shadows, keeping their distance. Ricardo walked into the hotel and sat down in one of the chairs in the foyer. He grabbed a magazine and started thumbing through the pages. In about five minutes, two other men showed up and sat down next to Ricardo. This time the two men who had joined Ricardo were now looking around to see who was in the room. Miguel looked at Lucas. "I don't like the feel of this; something is wrong."

Lucas nodded. "It looks like a hit about to go down."

Miguel and Lucas worked their way around to the back of the hotel and came through the back door. Positioning themselves with a clear line of fire, they waited to see what would happen next. In a short time a man showed up with a couple of women hanging off his arms. Seeing Ricardo there, he froze and started to back out the door. The two girls with him, sensing something bad, moved away from him, screaming. This alerted Ricardo and his friends sitting in the foyer.

Ricardo was the first to get up and move towards the door. The other two followed him, covering each side of the door when Ricardo went out. The man they were after was hiding behind a stairwell in the shadows. Not seeing him, Ricardo's friends started moving down the street in opposite directions, looking for the man. Ricardo stood in the street, yelling for the man to come out, "Hey, Miguel, come on out, you dog; you know why we're here, don't you?"

As the man tried to escape he caught the eye of one of Ricardo's friends who then dragged him out into the middle of the street. By now, the man was kneeling in front of Ricardo, begging not to be killed. Ricardo started talking to the man. "You have said some bad things about the boss and you need to be taught a lesson on respecting your betters."

The man started crying and was grabbing Ricardo's leg, begging not to be shot. Ricardo laughed. "You are a dog licking my boots."

With that, Ricardo hit him in the face; this sent the man flying backwards onto the street.

While all of this was going on, Miguel and Lucas moved forward out of the hotel and onto the street, hiding behind two large potted plants as they continued watching the scene before them. The man, now lying on his back, tried to get up; but Ricardo's friends held him in place. Ricardo looked at the man lying there on the ground and was raising his gun to fire. Lucas shot

Ricardo in the head with his weapon. Ricardo fell to the ground, never knowing what hit him. Ricardo's friends, standing there for a moment in confusion, were cut down by Miguel. It was over in about 30 seconds and the man lying on the ground didn't know whether to run or thank his benefactors for what they had done. Lucas went over to the man and helped him get on his feet. The man looked at Lucas and Miguel. "Thank you for saving my life."

Miguel was checking the bodies to make sure they were dead and looking for anything that may be helpful to them. "Why do these men want to kill you?" Lucas asked.

"I stood up to them in a town council meeting the other day, and they don't like that."

"What would make you do something like that?" asked Miguel.

"They killed my brother for being related to the mayor."

"You, the mayor of the town?" asked Lucas.

"Yes, I am. I am the sixth one this year, so far," the man said, looking around.

"Well, we better get these bodies out of the middle of the street and hide them before anybody else shows up," said Lucas.

It took them a couple of minutes to move the bodies to the alleyway. After disposing of the bodies they went the mayor's house. The mayor showed Lucas and

Miguel to his kitchen so he could make them some coffee and get them off the streets for the night. The mayor was almost tripping over himself to thank Miguel and Lucas for saving him by offering them anything they wanted. Miguel contacted Fernando to let him know where they were and to go ahead and meet them at the mayor's house as soon as possible.

Chapter IV

Frankie, the Boss, was sitting in his jail cell reading a book when the prison guard came to his cell. "You have a visitor. Open cell door 324," he said through the radio he had on.

Frankie, putting his book down, waited as the prison guard opened his cell door. The prison guard, using his radio again, called the control center and told the manager to close cell door 324. After the door closed, Frankie rolled his wheelchair to the next set of doors, and as he did so the guard would call on his radio and have the doors opened in front of them and closed behind them, sequentially. Arriving at the visitors center, Frankie went to one of the windows and picked up the phone. The man on the other side of the glass picked up his phone. "Hey, Frankie, I got some good news for you."

"You found them?" Frankie asked.

"Yes, we did. They live in Arizona and have a son working for the Phoenix Police Department, as well," said the man.

"Good, you know what you need to do," Frankie said, as he smiled.

"We'll take care of it, Frankie; don't you worry about

it anymore," the man said.

As the man left the visitors center, Frankie thought to himself, smiling for the first time in the three years being in prison, *"I'm going to do to you the same thing you did to me and more. I just wish I could be there to do it myself."*

Frankie yelled for the guard to come to take him back to his cell. He was smiling as he left the visitors center, and as he made his way to his cell he started to laugh, thinking to himself, *"Finally, payback for the life that was taken from me, I will take your life and everything in it that matters to you. You'll regret the day you did this to me."*

The man left the prison for the parking lot and made his way to his car. Once inside the car, he made a phone call and left a message to get the ball rolling. He hung up his phone and drove his car out of the prison parking lot onto I-15 and headed back to Las Vegas. The wheels were in motion and the time was near for Frankie.

Foster, who was home early for the weekend, had gathered up his fishing pole and gear and was headed out the door with his wife and kids to their favorite spot on Lake Pleasant. The boat was hooked up to the truck and the kids were waiting patiently in the truck, with Foster's wife, Elaine, locking the door to the house behind her. As Elaine got into the truck and was putting on her seatbelt, Foster's cell phone rang. He looked at Elaine as he answered the phone. "This had better be important."

The voice on the other end said, "It is boss. Sorry to call you so late on Friday, but something has come up and we need you to come back into the office for a minute."

"Can't it wait till Monday?" Foster said, almost pleading with the voice on the other end.

The voice started laughing. "I got you, boss."

Foster looked relieved, and then mad at the caller. "When I come in, I want to see you first thing Monday morning."

The voice on the other end of the phone laughed. "I'm not worried; you'll have forgotten by Monday, old man."

Foster realized who it was by now and chuckled to himself. "Buck, you son of a gun, how are you?"

"I thought I'd call and see what you're doing now that you're the big man on campus in the big world of the Arizona Bureau of Investigation."

"As a matter of fact, I gave myself Friday off to go fishing with my family. Being a boss, I can do those things nowadays."

"We'll, when you get back from your fishing trip, how about we get together and share some war stories?"

"I might need that, if I don't get going here. The wife and kids are getting fidgety and we haven't even pulled out of the driveway yet. I'll call you Monday and we'll set up a time and place to get together."

"Works for me; we'll talk to you on Monday."

After Buck hung up the phone, Foster looked at Elaine and said as he pulled out of the driveway in front of his house, "You remember the guy I worked with on the case involving the bank robbery…," telling her the story all the way down to the lake.

They arrived at Lake Pleasant in about an hour and the camp was set up in 20 minutes, with the kids pitching in to help. Foster had the boat in the water in another 15 minutes and was sitting in it when Elaine called everybody for dinner. With the sun going down in the west, the sky was lit up in different shades of orange clouds and blue sky. The heat of the day was starting to dissipate. By midnight it would be only 100 degrees and starting to cool down for the night.

The Intel section of the bureau of prisons had taken a picture of the man who had visited Frankie earlier that day. Using facial-recognition software, Mike Jones loaded the picture of the man into the computer and let the computer do its magic. Within fifteen minutes the computer stopped running and sent a signal to Mike that they had found a hit for the picture. Mike walked over to the computer and looked at the information and the picture on the computer screen. He wrote it down and sent the information to the FBI office in Las Vegas. As Mike was leaving for the weekend, he turned off the lights to his computer room and walked down the hall to the exit. He left the building and, heading back to

Las Vegas, was thinking about having a good time spending some of his money at the 21 tables in the Silver Slipper Casino Saturday night. The information sent to the FBI office would be there to be reviewed on Monday morning by one of the agents in the office.

Buck and Rachael were set to go for the weekend to drive over to Phoenix to see their grandkids and spend the weekend with Marissa. With Miguel being gone, Marissa was open for some company from Buck and Rachael, not only to see them, but to help her with the kids, which was always a nice relief for her. And being able to talk to some adults was a definite plus. Some much needed down time was always appreciated by Marissa, by having grandma and grandpa around for the kids.

Evans and Linda, with the weekend coming, decided to head to St. George, Utah, to get away from the heat and visit Zion Canyon to see the mountains and the rivers of southern Utah. Having Linda's parents come down to watch little Evan for the weekend would be Linda's and Evans' first break they've had in two months to be by themselves. Getting out of the heat and into the mountains would be a nice change of pace for them, and they were looking forward to it. Staying at the Ramada Inn hotel in St. George for the weekend was an ideal getaway. Having a pool there, the water was actually cool and felt good as they relaxed while waiting for dinner. Later that evening they would catch a show at the Tuacahn Theater on Friday night and then head into Zion National Park on Saturday.

With the weekend set for all involved, everybody was off to have some fun, to get away from the pressures of life. Each of them knew Monday morning would bring some of life's reality back into focus.

As the plane taxied to terminal gate A-3 at McCarren International Airport, two men sat waiting for the stewardess of Delta flight 231 to open the door to let the passengers start filing off the airplane and through the aircraft walkway. The flight had originated in Chicago with a stop in Denver to pick up more passengers for the final leg to Vegas.

The two men who got off the flight, Joey and Vincent, were met by John, who provided transportation for the two of them back to the Frontier Hotel. John made sure Joey and Vincent were taken care of for food and drink while at the Frontier Hotel and even had a car ready for their use for traveling. He also made sure that their hotel in Phoenix was paid for with the extra stuff that Joey had asked for. They would only be in Vegas for a short time before heading to Phoenix to take care of the hit on Buck and Rachael before heading back to Vegas to catch their return flight to Chicago. With that thought in mind, Joey and Vincent headed down into the casino to try their luck at craps.

The airport security monitor at McCarren International watched the passengers feed into the terminal from the different gates, all the while the computer was taking pictures of their faces for facial recognition to see who was coming into town that might be a problem later on. This information was fed to the Metro Police Department to be reviewed by Metro's Intel division. Joey and Vincent would be found in their files and then the Intel personnel would be alerted, and their information would be sent to the FBI office, as well.

Frankie just sat in the wheelchair and smiled, knowing that the world was about to change for Buck and Rachael like it had for him that evening when he first met them. The prison in Frankie's mind was bigger and the walls thicker than the one he sat in for the last three years. He looked around the cell, wondering if there would ever be a chance for him to leave this physical prison and walk out a free man again. The FBI had offered to put him into the witness-protection program by having him inform on his counterparts throughout the United States. He had refused to say anything that would benefit him or the FBI when it came to what he knew. This is the price he was willing to pay to stay alive in the system of smoke and mirrors. The lies and a lack of trust that was part of the Organization he had worked for had come at a high price. By being in prison and out of the way, he was still alive and that was better than it had been for some of his former clients that were caught lying by the

Organization.

Chapter V

Monday morning came too soon for all involved. The trip to St George was scenic, nice and cool. The grandkids were as cute as ever and the fishing trip was what was needed for a break from the job. The fish Foster caught gave him something to brag about to his coworkers at the office and kept getting bigger each time he told the story.

Upon arriving at the office in Las Vegas, Evans was reviewing the latest Intel about the comings and goings of the people who arrived at the airport and who visited whom in the prison. After looking at Joey and Vincent, drinking his second cup of coffee, Evans called Linda in to take a look at their photos. Linda came in smiling. "What can I do for you this morning?"

"Take a look at these pictures and see if they ring a bell to you," Evans said.

"These are professional hit men working for the Organization based in Chicago," she said as she laid the pictures down on the desk. "I wonder what they're doing here in Vegas?"

"Now take a look at this picture."

Again, looking at the other picture handed to her, she sat down and tried to remember who he was. "I know this guy; we've run into him before, but I can't remember where or when."

"He used to work for Frankie at the Frontier Hotel on the Strip."

"Yes, that's right, now I remember. Where was this taken again?"

"At the state prison south of here. His name is Monty, and he was a fixer for Frankie, a kind of a wise guy."

"Two paid assassins and a wise guy showing up in our photo collection. I wonder what this means?"

"Nothing good, I can tell you; these people don't show up and get together unless there is a reason."

"I agree, but who is their target and why?"

"I wonder if this may have something to do with some noise coming off the street about something big going to happen."

"Yes, but the impression I get is it's not happening here in town. We need to check our confidential informants (CI's) and see if we can shake something loose."

"I'll get the Special Agents in Charge in the southwest region in Phoenix and let them know what's happening."

"I'll check with Metro and see if anything has come through on their end and I'll pass it on to our friends and neighbors in California, Arizona, and Utah."

Foster came back to work on Monday morning all relaxed and ready to start the day. After having his first cup of coffee the briefing began about the weekend activities. There were two homicides over the weekend, both gang related, and a drug bust that netted ten kilos of heroin along with the distributor, and a car wreck involving three cars on the 101 route. No one was hurt badly, but it took two hours to clean it up, all in all, a quiet weekend. With the briefings done and no one scheduled to come in, Foster picked up his phone and called Buck.

After the third ring on Buck's cell phone, he answered the phone, "Hello."

"Yes, I would like to order a double-cheese pizza with anchovies on it," Foster said.

"I'm sorry, you have the wrong number."

"Oh, it is? Well, in that case, can I talk to your boss?"

"I am the boss."

"You are? What kind of place do you have there, telling me you don't sell pizzas?"

There was a pause; then Buck said, "Hey, Foster, what's up?"

"Nothing," he said, laughing. "I was just returning your call from Friday."

"Rachael and I were thinking of coming over to see you guys some weekend. How does that sound to you guys?"

"Fine, maybe we could get some fishing in while we're together. That way the ladies and the kids could play, as well, and leave the manly stuff for us to do,"

Foster said, smiling.

"Works for me. What's your schedule like for next week?"

"Next week is good for us. My mother-in-law won't be around for another week or two," Foster said, laughing.

"Mine either, for that matter." Buck laughed as Rachael walked into his office.

"Fine, then we'll see you Friday afternoon around four o'clock at your place."

"Be there or be square," Foster replied, "and bring some coats; you know how cold it gets in the mountains."

"Oh yeah, it's supposed to snow everywhere but here," Buck said, laughing.

After Buck hung up he looked at Rachael. "Hello, grandma."

Rachael smiled. "Sexy senior citizen to you, mister."

"Oh yes, I forgot." Buck chuckled at her remark.

"We just got this off the wire from our friends in Las Vegas," Rachael said. "It's an alert on two known hit men landing in Las Vegas and one of Frankie's boys having a meeting with Frankie at the prison."

"Well, how is our wheelchair-bound friend in prison doing?" Buck asked, not expecting an answer.

Rachael had a bad feeling in the pit of her stomach. "I have a bad feeling about this and these two guys, Buck."

Buck paused for a moment. "We need to be extra

careful until we know what they're up to."

"We need to be extra careful especially with the kids, Marissa and our grandkids," Rachael agreed.

Buck got up and walked over to Rachael and held her. "Until we know more we need to be sure before we go off halfcocked. I'll call Marissa and tell her to be careful."

"I'll call her; it will sound better coming from me than you."

"As you wish. Try not to scare her."

"Why do you think I'm telling her, instead of you?" she said, smiling.

"Women, you can't shoot them, and you can't live without them," Buck said, smiling.

Rachael left the room laughing and as Buck sat back down in his chair he thought to himself out loud, *"What are you up to, Frankie, and does it involve Rachael and me?"*

Joey and Vincent got a late start going to Phoenix on Monday and were still loading the car with their suitcases. Once done, they stopped and got some gas to fill up their tank. As they drove on Lake Mead Boulevard toward Hoover Dam, they crossed the bridge that spanned the gorge to the Arizona side. Arriving in Phoenix in the evening, they paid for a hotel room and stayed the night there. The next morning they would be in Smith County and looking for their quarry to finish the contract.

Buck called Evans in Las Vegas to follow up on the

information he had sent out earlier in the day. Evans answered the phone. "I wondered when you would call about this."

"What do you make of it so far?"

"We don't know at this point."

"Rachael has a bad feeling about this one."

"I do, too; the word from our sources say it isn't here in Vegas the hit will take place. Let me do some checking at the prison for you, and if anything comes up I'll let you know."

"Thanks and say hi to Linda and little Evan for us, will you."

"Will do, and back at you for Rachael and the kids' goodbye."

As Foster was reviewing the photos he had received from the Las Vegas FBI, he recalled what he had learned about the situation that Buck and Rachael found themselves in while in Las Vegas. They were still talking about the three FBI agents that were shot, two of whom died, with one of the dead agents being corrupt; also, the outcome from the legal proceedings for all the players that got caught in the end. He knew it would be just a matter of time before any of them would seek revenge, if and when they got the chance to even the score for being incarcerated because of Rachael and Buck. He knew it was inevitable for someone to do something for what they had done to the Organization and the drug trade in California.

Foster, just to be safe, called down to the Highway Patrol office in Smith County and left a message for the troopers working that area of Arizona to keep an eye on Buck and Rachael in their patrols down there. Five minutes later the message was received, understood and sent back to confirm its receipt.

Marissa took the news from Rachael very well and knew that if there were any problems for her and the kids, Buck and Rachael would be there in no time at all.

Miguel's boss, Special Agent Smith, received the information from the Las Vegas FBI office about the two hit men arriving in Las Vegas via the airport, and wondered if it had anything to do with Miguel's stepparents. Not knowing for sure, he thought it was better to be safe than sorry by keeping an eye on Marissa and the kids for Miguel.

For all involved it was a matter of waiting and seeing what would turn up. For Joey and Vincent it was another day in the lives of killers waiting to strike.

Chapter VI

Miguel and Lucas met up with Fernando later that
night at the mayor's house. As they sat there drinking
their coffee trying to come up with a plan to get into the
cartel house, they reviewed different scenarios
throughout the night. The mayor was able to give them
information about the route the truck took to get food
and the girls for the guards. It seems that the truck
made a stop at the local Wal-Mart for food and toiletries
for the cartel house. The girls were found on the street
from one of the local pimps. This all occurred usually
on Wednesday, picking up the food first and then the
girls last. The truck would come into town and start
about nine o'clock in the morning and be back by four
o'clock in the afternoon. The rest of that afternoon,
when the truck got back, was spent having a party with
the girls and the guards that weren't on duty. Miguel
decided that would be the best time to try to get into the
compound and get the hard drive. Lucas agreed.
"With the men being busy, having fun with the girls and
drinking, the distraction would work in our favor."

So that being decided on, all they had to do was

figure out a time on Wednesday to hijack the truck on its weekly run.

When they left the mayor's house, they headed back to their hotel room and, staying in the shadows, were able to elude any cartel soldiers patrolling the streets. Miguel, thinking about their plan, wanted to check in with Smith and let him know that all was going according to schedule. Having reached Smith by the satphone on the following Sunday night, he relayed the message to Smith about their plan. Not getting into the details, Miguel let him know they were getting ready to go in and get the computer. Smith liked the gist of the plan and said, "Be careful out there."

"That was the most important part of the plan," Miguel said.

After settling down for the night, they could hear gunfire coming from the part of town where they had just come from.

The next day the paper read that the mayor had been killed in his house late Saturday night. Miguel wondered if the mayor had kept quiet about their plans for going into the cartel house. Time would tell whether he had talked or not.

Taking in some of the sites around the city, they waited until Wednesday morning at the Wal-Mart for the red pickup truck to show. At nine-thirty it showed up on its regular run for food. Miguel and Lucas walked into Wal-Mart and started following the guards, who were buying the food for the cartel. There were a total of three of them in the store with baskets for the food they were buying. Each had a list of things to pick up for each basket. Miguel looked at Lucas. "It's amazing how some things are the same, no matter what country you're in. I guess shopping for food is the same anywhere you go."

Lucas nodded and laughed at the men doing the shopping, pushing their baskets all over Wal-Mart.

In a couple of hours the baskets were full of food, and the men were standing in line to pay for what they had picked up. Fernando was outside in the red pickup they got from Ricardo and his friends. When Miguel and Lucas came out of the store, they looked for Fernando, finding him, they walked over to the truck. Getting in, they left immediately to position themselves in front of the cartel truck, so they could hijack the truck before they picked up the girls. About 100 yards from Wal-Mart, Lucas and Miguel got out and raised the hood on the red truck they were driving. Parked in such a way that the cartel truck couldn't go around them, it stopped and two of the guards got out of the truck and started cussing at Lucas and Miguel, trying to get them to move their truck. Fernando, who was watching from the sidewalk, went over and stuck a gun in the cartel driver's face, "Don't do anything to upset me or my friends."

The two guards nearest Miguel and Lucas were still

yelling when they were knifed and dragged to the back of Ricardo's truck and thrown in the bed. Miguel and Lucas came from behind Ricardo's truck after dumping the bodies and jumped into the red cartel truck and said to the driver, "Move!" Fernando got the other truck out of the way and drove off in another direction out of town with the bodies in the back of the truck.

Lucas, pretending to be a guard, went to where they were to pick up the girls. He started talking to the pimp, offering money for the girls for the night. The pimp was shaking his head and asking for more money, and after reaching a price the pimp told the girls to get in the back of the truck and he would see them tomorrow. With girls and food in the back of the truck, Lucas and Miguel, along with the driver, headed back to the cartel house. Wearing the dead men's hats and bandanas, they looked the part of being guards. About five miles from the cartel house they had the driver stop the truck and get out. They took his boots and hat from him and made him walk back the five miles to town. As he was leaving, Miguel shot him in the leg so that it would be a while before he got to town. Miguel, in order not to arouse the suspicion of the girls in the back of the truck, cussed at him for being so stupid and forgetting his shoes when they didn't have time to go back and get them for him. The girls were afraid at first, but by the time Miguel quit cussing the man out, they all were laughing at him for being stupid. Everything went back to normal for the girls, who were now looking forward to the party that was about to happen at the cartel house.

When Miguel and Lucas got to the front gate, the guards waved them in and were catcalling the girls in the back of the truck. They drove through the gate and stopped in front of the house and started unloading the food and the girls. The guards, who were off duty, helped with the girls and took off with them in all directions. The booze was also unloaded and taken by the off-duty guards, as well. Fortunately, Lucas and Miguel grabbed two of the bottles and kept them for themselves.

By now the food was put away and the party was starting. The music was loud in the house and the guards' quarters, as well. Miguel and Lucas moved around the house, looking for the computer laptop, and went from room to room to do so. Whenever they ran into somebody, they feigned being drunk and unaware of where they were at. Finding the main office, they rummaged through the desk until they found a button inside one of the drawers. Pushing the button, another door opened behind a wall. Lucas walked through the door while Miguel stood guard, and after five minutes Lucas came out with the hard drives from the two computers he had found in the room. Closing the door, they retreated back to the front of the house. Leaving the house, they walked into the compound area and slowly made their way to the front gate. The guards were wondering what Miguel and Lucas were doing there, until they offered their bottles to them. The guards, looking around, making sure they were not seen drinking, took big swallows from the bottles. They handed them back to Lucas and Miguel, who in turn would look like they were drinking from the bottles and would hand them back to the guards, who took heavy hits from the bottles again and again. Finally, the guards at the gate refused to give the bottles back to Miguel and Lucas. Miguel and Lucas offered to take their place as guards so that they could join the party in the compound. The gate guards gladly gave up their post and, handing their guns to them, quickly made their way to the party to join in the fun, at the same time saying thank you to Miguel and Lucas for helping at the front gate. After five minutes, the party inside the compound was at a fever pitch. Seeing that the time to go was now, Miguel locked the gate from the outside and he and Lucas left the compound with the hard drives in their pockets and headed off into the desert.

Traveling through the desert and staying off the road was their only chance of getting away from the cartel gunmen, once they realized what had happened. Miguel and Lucas kept below the ridge line of the mountains and carefully worked their way back to Culiacan. Arriving there at night, they met up with Fernando at the hotel. Once there, Fernando drove them to the airport.

Dropping off the truck at the airport parking lot, Miguel and Lucas were trying to buy some time before the cartel would be looking for them. Miguel went into the airport for a couple of minutes to see if there was anything available for them to fly. Coming back after five minutes, shaking his head, they headed into the desert for the trip back to America.

As the party continued throughout the night for the men at the cartel compound, it wasn't until the next morning they realized that someone had been there that wasn't supposed to be. The driver that Miguel shot had arrived back in town and had called the cartel house to warn them. But by then it was too late for the guards to do anything about it.

Most of the men were still either drunk or hung over from the party. After searching the compound they couldn't find anything wrong, which for the cartel boss didn't make any sense at all. The cartel boss asked himself why anybody would break into the compound and not take anything. As far as he could tell at first glance, everything was in its place and nothing was missing.

Even after looking at his computers behind the wall door, it wasn't until the cartel boss tried to use his computers that he realized the hard drives were missing. This infuriated him, that the hard drives had been stolen, since all of his information for running the cartel was on those hard drives. He knew that there was enough information on the hard drives to destroy his whole operation or, worse yet, put him in jail. As far as the he was concerned, those hard drives had to be found or be destroyed.

The gunmen found the truck that Fernando had left at the airport. At first, the boss and his men thought that the thieves had flown out of the Culiacan airport. It was only after checking with the airport personnel that the cartel boss realized it was just a trick to throw them off their scent. He realized that Miguel and Lucas were on foot or had found another car to leave the city. Splitting his men into two teams, he sent one team through the desert, and the other team in a truck down the highway searching for the two men and the hard drives. The team that was tasked to go in the desert was not sure where to start. Fanning out in a 180-degree arc, they moved forward, starting at the airport. In about an hour one of the guards whistled for the team leader to come over. Upon getting there, he could see footprints in the sand and, following them a little ways, was sure they were the footprints of the two men they were looking for.

"We have footprints leading into the desert, and I'm pretty sure they are of the two we're looking for," he said, calling the boss to let him know of their find.

"Continue, I'll send the rest of the team in your direction from the other side and catch them in the middle," the cartel boss replied.

Still moving through the desert, Miguel and Lucas were making good time. Fernando was a little slower and needed more rest, simply because of his age and the pace that they were going. Miguel sat and waited with Lucas for Fernando to catch up to them. Finally, stopping to catch his breath, Fernando said, "I'm slowing you down; leave me or you'll never get out of here alive."

"Nonsense. We came together, we get out of this together," said Miguel.

Lucas looked at Fernando. "I've got an idea. How about we send Fernando on a different trail and we keep going on from here?"

Miguel and Fernando looked at him, wondering what he was talking about.

"How about we find a place for Fernando to slip away and head to the highway and get to Nogales to send the cavalry to the rescue? All we need to do is make sure he's not followed."

"How do we do that?" asked Miguel.

"We create a distraction to keep them on our trail instead of Fernando's. Right now, all they know is that there are only two of us working this, not three of us. It'll be easier for Fernando to get away than have him get caught with us," Lucas said, thinking out loud.

As Miguel was thinking about it, Fernando said, "Sounds like a plan to me."

"Plus, if we give the hard drives to Fernando, I'm pretty sure he'll get through better than we would," Lucas said.

"We need to keep the hard drives with us, but if Fernando can get to the highway, he can get to Smith and ask him for help," Miguel said.

Fernando and Lucas agreed with Miguel, and they all started back on the trail, looking for a rock outcropping where Fernando could slip away without leaving any footprints to follow. In about 20 minutes they found what they were looking for, a layer of rock that went for quite a distance towards the direction of the highway. After saying their goodbyes and good luck, they parted ways. Lucas and Miguel were able to make better time now since splitting up, and Fernando was out of sight within a quarter mile.

Lucas and Miguel made some big trails for the cartel men to follow so that they would take the heat off Fernando as he made his way to the highway. The cartel leader sent his best trackers forward, and they were about 200 yards in front of the other men. The trackers would send signals to their teammates to tell them where they were.

Miguel was watching from a ridge with Lucas. "We need to get those trackers off our backs, and I have an idea of what to do."

"Care to fill me in?" asked Lucas.

"I want you to attract their attention and bring them

up this way toward you, and I'll come up behind them and disable them. All we need to find is a narrow canyon or wash."

"You mean like that one over there?" Lucas asked, pointing in the direction of the rock wall.

"That'll do just fine. Give me a couple of minutes to get set up and you can make a noise to get them over there by the wall."

At the base of the rock wall was a dry riverbed that hadn't seen rain in a while. Climbing up about ten feet on the face of the wall, Lucas waited a couple of minutes to start making noises by throwing rocks down the face of the rock wall. One of the trackers heard the noise and signaled his partner to follow him to the rock wall. By now Miguel was moving around them and was able to get behind them. Slowly following the two trackers, he moved closer to the trailing tracker. The trackers were not concerned about anything behind them with the noise that Lucas was making. They were concentrating on finding the cause of the noise and, seeing Lucas, they started to move faster. Miguel was able to sneak up on the one tracker, who was behind the first one. Grabbing the tracker by the mouth, he snapped his neck, killing him instantly. The second tracker never made a sound as Miguel laid him carefully in a depression on the desert floor. The first tracker lost sight of Lucas and had to stop in order to find him again. He continued working his way up to the rock face of the mountain.

Lucas got down off of the rock face and hid in the dry riverbed closest to the tracker, waiting for him to appear. Occasionally, he would throw a rock to keep the tracker coming forward toward him. The tracker turned around at one point and found he was all alone. As he was not able to see his partner and sensing something wasn't right, he turned around and headed back to the main group of searchers. Miguel was waiting for him just over the next rise. As the tracker was making his way back down, Lucas followed him down the mountain, keeping a safe distance and out of sight. The tracker looked down below him and saw something lying in the desert that wasn't normal. As he got closer, the tracker recognized his partner lying there. He looked around and wasn't sure which way to run, up or down the mountain. As he stood there a moment trying to decide, Miguel came up from behind, buried his knife into the base of the skull, and twisted the blade. The tracker went limp like a rag doll, and Miguel lay the tracker down on the ground next to his partner.

By now, Lucas was standing next to Miguel. "Man, you have all the fun. Next time it's my turn, you hear me?"

"Okay, I promise; next time it's your turn," Miguel said, smiling.

Grabbing the two canteens from the dead trackers, the two started off again toward the mountains.

As the two of them made their way on the trail, they

made up for the lost time by jogging a mile or so. The team of guards found their trackers lying on the ground and started getting nervous about where the two men they were tracking could be. Manuel, the leader of the group, called the cartel boss and let him know that his two trackers were dead and asked, "What do you want us to do?"

"Keep going after them and when you find them, bring them both to me!" said the cartel boss, hanging up the phone.

Manuel called the other team leader in the field and let him know what had happened to his trackers. Ricci, the other leader, replied, "Not to worry; we'll find them for you."

With the phone calls complete, the two cartel teams started moving in towards one another, hoping to eventually catch Lucas and Miguel in the middle.

From their vantage point Lucas and Miguel could see the valley below for miles, and sitting there catching their breath, Miguel spotted some movement coming from the north along the desert floor below them. Pointing this out to Lucas, they made their way higher into the mountains. Finding an old waterfall in the rocks, they climbed up into the shadows and continued watching the valley below. Miguel looked at Lucas. "How do you want to play this?"

"We could go down there and raise hell with the teams while they are looking for us. That sounds like fun to me," Lucas replied.

"We have plenty of water to last us for a couple more days; we just need some food to get us by," Miguel said as he checked the canteens for water.

"How about we go down there and get the truck following them and hijack it and then drive to Hermosillo? That way the men out there will be stuck with no food or water and will have to call off the search for us."

Miguel thought about this for a minute, "Lucas, I think you might have the right idea on handling this."

"Naturally I have," Lucas said. Miguel looked at him and smiled while Lucas laughed.

Lucas and Miguel made their way across the mountain and got behind the team led by Manuel. The truck was slowing making its way through the desert to keep up with the team. The truck was carrying the water and food to sustain the men as they searched the desert. Because of the weight of the truck, it was constantly getting stuck in the sand, and the two men who stayed with the truck had to keep moving it past the sand piles. By now, the team was moving faster than the truck could, and were eventually out of sight of the truck.

Lucas and Miguel were starting to make their descent down from the mountain and eventually made their way behind the truck. Coming up on the truck, seeing that it was stuck again in the sand, they offered to assist in getting the truck unstuck. The two men thought Lucas and Miguel were part of the team and gladly accepted their help. Once the truck was able to move again and was slowly driving through the desert, Miguel and Lucas followed behind the two men, killing them with their knives. The driver of the truck was so busy trying to keep the truck from getting stuck again that he failed to see what had happened to the men. Lucas came up to the driver in the truck, who was slowly picking his way between the piles of sand and stuck a gun in his face and ordered the man to stop the truck and get out, which the driver did. And as he was standing there, Miguel cold-cocked him and tied him up, leaving him to figure out how to survive in the desert by himself.

Lucas and Miguel got in the truck, turned it around and headed toward the highway. Only getting the truck stuck once, they made it to the highway and started traveling toward Hermosillo. The teams eventually met in the desert later in the evening, and having no luck finding the two men, they headed back towards the truck, which they expected to be behind Manuel's team. After walking an hour in the desert, they couldn't find the truck. Running low on water and not knowing what happened to the truck, the men started to panic. Manuel had to fire his gun into the air in order to regain control of the group of men. Walking to Culiacan City was a tortuous five miles back through the desert and they had no extra water, only what they were carrying. The men started arguing about being thirsty, especially the ones who didn't have their own canteens. The men who had the canteens refused to share their water with the ones who didn't. This would start off as a fight and then gunfire would erupt and whoever won the gunfight got or kept the water. This happened twice before Manuel and Ricci took all of the canteens and started carrying them.

By now, Lucas and Miguel were on their way to Hermosillo and ready to take a plane out of the city. They stopped once to send a message to Smith to let him know they were on their way back to Nogales. Smith acknowledged the message, "I'll be waiting for you and your next call to pick you up."

Smith debated whether or not to tell Miguel about the hit man from Las Vegas that were sent by Frankie. Not knowing who the target was, he decided to wait until he had further information that would confirm who the target was, hoping and praying that he was making the right decision for his team.

Chapter VII

Joey and Vincent sat in the diner having breakfast and talking amongst themselves about where to look for Buck and Rachael. Joey offered an idea. "Maybe we find the daughter-in-law and follow her; she may lead us to our targets."

"There's no guarantee that will work; besides, we know where they live already," Vincent said as he drank his coffee.

"Yeah, you're right," said Joey, continuing, "Frankie wanted us to take the whole family out too, remember?"

Vincent nodded his head and thought about what Joey had just said. Putting down his fork and wiping his hands on the napkin, he said, "Let's go after the kids first and then that will draw out the parents and we'll get them."

Joey smiled and started to drink his coffee and eat his breakfast. When Joey and Vincent were done with breakfast, they left the diner and went out to their car and drove away. Joey, who was driving, asked Vincent, "Do we have an address for the kids?"

Vincent thumbed through his I-phone and brought up the address of where the kids lived in the city. "It says here that they live in Glendale at 6042 Prickly Pear Dr., off the 101 loop."

"Point me in the right direction," said Joey as he put the car into gear.

Finding their way onto the 101 loop, they headed to 75th Avenue and took the exit from the loop, going through Peoria, and then made their way to Happy Valley Road and took a left turn on 67th Avenue and started looking for the address of the house. Using GPS, they found the address of the house but couldn't go into the subdivision because it was gated. Joey looked around, realizing that there was no way in, got out of the car and walked over to the gate and stood there. After about five minutes of looking around, Vincent honked the horn and motioned for Joey to come back to the car. Vincent looked at Joey, "Try not to stand out like a sore thumb, will ya."

Joey looked at Vincent and nodded. "I guess you're right; sorry about that."

"Let's get out of here before somebody sees us and starts to wonder why we're sitting here."

Joey started the engine and drove off back towards the city of Glendale and stopped at a 7-11 to get something to drink for the both of them.

Marissa had just got out of the shower and was getting ready to feed the kids when Special Agent Smith called. "I apologize for calling today instead of waiting for Sunday. I wanted to just let you know that Miguel is all right and will be coming home shortly."

Marissa thanked him for the call and was about to hang up when Smith asked, "Do you need anything till Miguel gets back?" And added, "By the way, have you seen anything out of the ordinary lately?"

"No, I don't need anything, and I haven't seen anything unusual at all around here."

"Okay, just checking to be sure. I'll talk to you Sunday then. Goodbye."

"Goodbye," Marissa said, wondering what that was all about and thinking to herself, "Maybe I'd better call Buck and Rachael to see if they know something I don't know."

Hitting the express dial on her cell phone, she got hold of Rachael. "Is there anything wrong or going on that I need to be aware of?"

"Hi, first of all, and how are you doing?"

"Good, and the kids are fine, as well."

"We heard about two hit men we think were sent by Frankie, and they may be coming after us. However, that being said, we are not sure who their target is yet."

"Do you think they'll come after me and the kids to get to you?" Marissa asked nervously.

"We don't know anything for certain yet, but I suggest you stay in the house as much as you can; leastwise, until we have more information to go on. If need be, we'll come and get you and bring you down here to stay for a while."

"I'll do that, the kids are feeling a little sick this morning, anyway."

"Oh, I'm sorry; tell them Grandma hopes they start feeling better soon. We'll call you as soon as we find out anything new."

"All right. Thanks, Mom. We'll be in touch soon."

After hanging up, Marissa walked around the house and checked the front door and the back door to make sure they were locked. She then went to the kitchen to fix breakfast for the kids and continued getting dressed, as well. As she was getting dressed, she kept an eye on the street in front of her house and watched the cars and trucks that were driving by, making sure none of them stopped in front of her house; leastwise, the ones she didn't recognize.

Marissa wished that Miguel was here right now because he would know what to do. He always knew what to do in situations like this, she thought to herself. Now it was on her to figure out how to handle what might be coming. Looking through the drawer in the nightstand next to the bed, she pulled her nine mm semi-auto out of the drawer and chambered a round into the gun, put it on safety and slipped it into her pocket. She had learned to fire the gun at the insistence of Miguel, not only to protect herself but the children, for times like this. Marissa had never fired the gun, except at a target down range, but her accuracy was amazing to Miguel. She also knew shooting at a target was a lot different than shooting a real person in the heat of the moment. Hopefully, she wouldn't need to realize the difference between the two.

Rachael contacted Buck about the phone call from Marissa. "I'm wondering if we need to have Marissa and the grandkids come down and stay with us for a couple of days."

Buck, thought about what Rachael had said, "Knowing Frankie like we do, it could be that he wants to take the kids out to get to us, thereby drawing us out to catch us out in the open and kill us."

"Frankie would like to do that, just to make us hurt as much as he does because of being in a wheelchair. Do you think Foster could help us with this?"

"Too early to tell if it would be necessary to contact him at this point. Until we know for sure, I don't want to call him."

"I agree. Have we heard anything from Evans and Linda lately?"

"No, in fact, I was thinking about calling them today."

"Don't worry about it; I'll call them right now. Besides, I haven't talked to Linda in a while," Rachael said as she walked out of his office.

Rachael opened her cell phone and speed-dialed Linda's phone number. After ringing a couple of times Linda answered, "Hello, Linda speaking."

Rachael identified herself over the phone. "How's our godchild doing?"

"Little Evan is doing just fine, wondering when you're coming up to visit him."

"Maybe this winter, when we get some time off again."

"I'll tell him that maybe he'll see you this winter, then. What can I do for you?"

"I know Buck has talked to Evans already. I was just wondering if anything else has turned up since the last phone call."

"I don't know; let me check with Evans on it and I'll call you back, okay?"

"Fine; I'll talk to you shortly, then."

Linda went into Evans' office and told him about Rachael calling for an update. "The last word on the street is that they're nowhere to be found here in Vegas. All we know for sure is that they didn't fly out of McCarren airport," Evans said.

"They could be on the move, then, to parts unknown."

"I would think that if they're driving, it has to be close to Vegas or, otherwise, they would have flown to the city where the hit was to occur."

"How far is Phoenix from Las Vegas, anyway?"

"It's about five or six hours from here," Evans said, wondering if the drive was close enough for the two hit men to do it. "Let me call down to Phoenix and see if anything has come up out of the ordinary down there."

Picking up the phone, he called the Phoenix FBI office.

It only took about a minute to ask the right questions to the lead agent down there. "Have any of your agents picked up any information about two hit men being down there?" Evans asked.

"Not that I'm aware of. Let me check with some of my people here."

Evans could hear the agent in charge ask, "Has anything shook lose about the bulletin dealing with the two hit men being in Phoenix?"

One voice said, "There was some scuttlebutt out and about from my sources, saying something might be coming down here in town. Nobody knows for sure, just talk right now."

The agent in charge came back to the phone and repeated what Evans had already heard. "I don't know how much credibility there is in this, but to be safe I will keep an eye on it myself."

"Could you do me a favor? A friend of mine, who is the sheriff down in Smith County, has a son and daughter-in-law living in Glendale, and I think they could be targets for the hit," Evans explained.

"Do you have a name and an address for them?" asked the agent in charge.

"Miguel and Marissa Tanner. They live at 6042 Prickly Pear Trail in Glendale. The husband works for the Phoenix Police Department in their narcotics unit. At least, that is the last I heard about him."

"I'll follow up on this and we'll check it out and I'll let

you know."

"That would be great; thanks for your time and help."

The agent in charge called the narcotics unit in the Phoenix Police Department and connected with Chad, who was in command of the unit. After identifying himself as Special Agent in Charge Williams, he asked, "Do you have a Miguel working there in your unit?

"He was reassigned to work with you guys as a liaison under deep cover against the cartel in Mexico. Why, is there anything wrong?" Chad asked.

"No, just following up on a telephone inquiry. Thanks for your time," Williams said.

Williams called Smith into his office, "What do you know about this Miguel guy?"

"He works for me and is undercover right now with another character from the Border Patrol. Why? What's up?"

"I'm sure you saw the bulletin from the Las Vegas FBI office about the two hit- men flying into Vegas and then disappearing, didn't you?"

"Yes, I did. In fact, it was Miguel's stepparents who were involved with shutting down the drug operation in Las Vegas and catching the West Coast distributor in California and they were also responsible for shutting down the syndicate up there, as well."

"Oh, yes, I remember that now. It was his parents that did that?"

"It seems that one of Frankie's friends went after their

son, Miguel, while he was living in Las Vegas. In the meantime, Frankie put a hit out on both of his parents. After Miguel's parents visited with Frankie and convinced him to cancel the hit, it seems that Frankie is now confined to a wheelchair. Evidently, he had both kneecaps blown out, plus two of his own men were found dead in his penthouse."

"Man, if I was Frankie, I would want some payback after something like that happened to me," Williams said, smirking at what Smith had just told him.

"You want me to go and sit on their house for a bit tonight?" Smith asked Williams.

"Yeah, better do it just in case the hit men made it down here. Take Reynolds with you when you go."

"Roger that; I'll go get him and a car, too."

Williams left Smith's office and went back to his desk and called Evans back. Getting a hold of him he explained what he was doing to help Miguel and his family. Evans thanked him for his support and said goodbye.

Evans called Linda updated her regarding what was going on and to get in touch with Rachael to let her know what was happening. Linda contacted Rachael and waited for her to pick up. "That was fast. What did you find out?" Rachael said.

"There is some scuttlebutt on the streets in Phoenix about two hit men being there, nothing concrete, but still, it could be true. The Phoenix office of the FBI is going to follow up to make sure all is well by having a couple of agents sit on the house for a few nights, just to be safe."

"I want to say thank you for keeping us in the loop on this."

"You're welcome, we look forward to seeing you guys sometime this winter," Linda said as she hung up the phone.

Rachael walked into Buck's office and told him what Linda had said. Looking concerned about the whole issue, she asked Buck, "What shall we do now?"

Buck said without hesitating, "We need to get to Marissa's house, now."

Getting into one of the sheriff's unmarked cars, they took off with the lights on, doing about 90 miles per hour to get to Phoenix. While in the car, Rachael called Foster and explained what was going on and what they were doing."

"I'll meet you there at their place in Glendale," Foster said.

"We need you to go under cover and just keep an eye on the place, if you will. Be aware that the FBI is going to be there, as well."

"Roger Wilco." Hanging up the phone, he quickly got into his car and headed to Glendale.

Earlier in the day, Joey and Vincent were trying to figure out the best way to carry out the hit on Miguel and Marissa. Doing the hit in the middle of the day would be hard without being seen. At night would be better and easier to be concealed from prying eyes, getting past the gated entrance would also be easier. Darkness, in this case, would be their friend in accomplishing their deed. No one would know who it was and why it happened. It would be one of those senseless murders you read about or see on the news channel. Everybody in the homeowners' association would be up in arms thinking something like this could happen in a gated community. After a while the outrage would die down and life would go back to normal again, as if it had never happened, except in idle gossip from the people next door to the house where it actually had happened.

Joey and Vincent waited until it was dark, at the right time they would return to finish part one, which would put into motion part two, the hit against Buck and Rachael.

Frankie was waiting in his prison cell for the news of the hit being carried out and was smiling at the prospect of two generations of a family that would be gone, as if they had never existed. He wanted to pull the trigger himself and watch as they pleaded for their lives, smiling at them as he pulled the trigger and watched them die. But Frankie, sitting in his cell, knew that it couldn't be, so he would have to just enjoy knowing that he ordered the hit on a famous couple and their kids. For Frankie, it would have to do. It would make it easier knowing that he killed the people that put him in a wheelchair as he sat in prison for the rest of his life. Besides, how many life sentences can you serve if you keep killing people while you're in prison? Even the death sentence couldn't be worse than being confined to this damn wheelchair.

Buck and Rachael continued driving to Glendale, praying that they would get there in time and hoping they were wrong about their gut instinct. If they were wrong, they would tell Marissa that this was a surprise visit from Grandpa and Grandma to see the kids.

Agents Smith and Reynolds pulled up to the gated community entrance, and after contacting the president of the homeowners' association, they drove through the gate and parked a little farther down the street so as not to alarm anyone by their presence, still close enough to watch the house.

Foster was there in 30 minutes. Leaving his car outside the gate, he jumped over the fence and walked through the neighborhood. Looking all around, he found Smith and Reynolds sitting in their car and walked over and introduced himself to them. Flashing his badge, he visited with the two FBI agents for just a moment before moving on and finding a place closer to the house to sit and wait and watch for anything to happen.

Buck and Rachael showed up around eight o'clock that evening. After contacting Marissa on the phone to let her know that they were in the area and wanting to see the kids, she gave them the pin number for the gate. After driving through the area and parking on the other side of the street, they went into the house to stay the night. Marissa was more than happy to see them and was relieved that Buck and Rachael were there. Buck stepped out of the house and heard a voice coming from the shadows. "Nice night, isn't it?"

Recognizing the voice, Buck replied, "Sure is, and thank you for being here."

"Just make sure this doesn't mess up our fishing," replied Foster.

Buck smiled at hearing the comment, "Heaven forbid!" He then walked back into the house.

Joey and Vincent didn't realize it, but this would be their last day on earth. Their day of reckoning was at hand. The only question now was who else would be going with them to meet their maker. Only time would tell at this point.

After midnight, Joey and Vincent came back to the gated entrance and parked their car across the street so as not to attract any attention. Crossing the road and working their way over the cinderblock walls adjacent to the gate, they walked up the street looking for the address where Miguel and Marissa lived. Smith, seeing the two men walking up the street, woke up Reynolds and carefully got out of the car. As they made their way to the house, keeping an eye on the two men in front of them, Smith and Reynolds stayed in the shadows away from the street lamps. Foster was watching, as well, from behind some bougainvillea bushes that had grown wild.

Joey pointed out the address to Vincent, "This is the place."

Looking around and seeing no one in the area, they made their way across the front yard to the window and checked to see if it was locked. Buck and Rachael were up and sitting in the dark by the front-room window. Rachael got up and went over to the sliding glass door in the kitchen and leaned up against the wall and waited, ready for anything.

Joey sent Vincent around the side of the house and had him climb over the block wall into the backyard, carefully making his way to the glass door and checked it. Vincent could see that a broomstick handle was in the groove of the sliding glass door. Smith and Reynolds took positions across the street from the house behind some parked cars and waited. Foster, moving from behind the bushes, came out of the shadows and was up by the front door, watching.

Joey climbed over the block wall and went over to where Vincent was. At this point, Vincent looked at Joey with a look of, "*What do we do now*?" Joey, reaching into his coat pocket, pulled a glass-cutting tool out and set it up about midway between the floor and the lock on the glass door. Carefully cutting the glass, he reached in and removed the stick from the glass-door groove. Then unlocking the lock, Joey slid the door back.

By now, Buck was there with Rachael, waiting and watching the glass door being opened. Joey went in first and, standing against the open door, his silhouette was clear. Buck fired his gun and Joey hit the floor, dead, in the dining room. Vincent, seeing what happened, ran to the side of the house and climbed back over the block wall, running past Foster, who fired and missed hitting Vincent, who in turn fired in the direction of the noise. Being hit by Vincent's bullet, Foster fell to the ground. Still conscious, Foster lay there on the porch, waiting to see what Vincent's next move would be. Vincent, standing in the middle of the street, looked back at the front door of the house. He could see a form lying on the porch. He walked back over to the porch to see what he had hit, at this point Foster rose up and fired once, hitting Vincent in the shoulder. Vincent took off in the direction of the gate, by now Smith and Reynolds came from behind the cars across the street and started chasing Vincent. Smith yelled, "FBI, stop!"

Vincent turned around and fired at the two agents, his shots missing completely. Smith and Reynolds both knelt on the ground and fired their weapons at Vincent simultaneously, with their aims being deadly accurate. Only firing once each, the two bullets hit Vincent in the chest cavity. Being mortally wounded, Vincent tried to raise his gun and fire at the agents one more time. Unable to do so, due to the loss of blood, he squeezed a round off into the pavement in front of him and dropped to the ground, dead.

Smith said to Reynolds, "Go check him out; I'm going back to check on Foster, I think he's been hit."

By now, Buck and Rachael were out on the porch looking at Foster, who had been hit. He lay on the ground with Buck holding his head up. The shot had hit him in the stomach and you could tell he was in pain. Rachael had already called 911 and they were on their way. Foster looked up at Buck. "Did we get them?"

Buck looked at Smith, and as Smith nodded to Buck, he replied, "We got them both."

Foster smiled. "Well done."

The siren of the ambulance could be heard off in the distance as it made its way to the house. Buck looked at Foster, "Hang on; they're almost here."

"I'm not going anywhere; we still got to go fishing with the families this summer," said Foster, smiling weakly.

"That's right, Foster, you owe me a trip on your boat to your favorite fishing spot."

The city police had arrived and were doing crowd control and had started investigating the shooting by talking to Buck, Rachael, and the FBI agents.

By now, the ambulance was there, and the paramedics

were working on Foster to stabilize his life signs. Once that was completed they loaded him into the ambulance and took him to the emergency room at the hospital. The ER team was waiting for his arrival and rushed him into the operating room to stop the loss of blood and fix the damage the bullet had done to him and save his life. Rachael went with the ambulance and called Foster's wife, Elaine, from the ambulance to let her know what had happened.

After the ER team took Foster into the operating room, Elaine showed up five minutes later, and seeing Rachael standing in the waiting room, she rushed over to her. Rachael quickly hugged her as Elaine cried. After gaining her composure, Elaine finally asked Rachael, "Did they say what the prognosis was for him?"

"They didn't say anything as they wheeled him into the operating room. All we can do at this point is to wait and see."

Back at the house, Buck looked at Joey laying on the floor and reached down, took the ring off his middle finger and put it in his pocket. He then walked outside to where Vincent was laying on the road and reached down and took the ring off his finger, as well. Marissa and the kids were awakened by the sound of gunfire.

Marissa told the kids to stay in their rooms while she walked down the hallway into the dining room, where she saw Joey lying on the floor. At this time Buck was headed back into the house, seeing Marissa, he went over to her, "You need to stay out of here for a little bit until forensics gets her and does their job. The team should be here any minute and I'll let you know when they're done."

Marissa, shocked at what she saw, walked back to her bedroom, making sure the kids were safe.

Reynolds came to where Smith was standing. "The man dead in the street didn't have any ID on his body. We'll have to wait for the fingerprints to identify him. We have a meat wagon on the way for both of them."

Smith nodded. "That was too close for comfort."

"How's the other guy doing? Will he make it?

"Too early to tell at this point. I'm praying that he does make it."

"Me too."

After the forensics team completed their picture taking and fingerprinting and everybody was gone, Buck told Marissa that everybody had left, and the house was back to being hers again. With the exception of the blood spot on the carpet and perfectly round hole in the sliding glass door, everything looked normal once again. Marissa, seeing the blood stain, stood there in shock and looking at Buck asked, "Were they here to kill me and the kids?"

"Yes, they were. Remember the man down in Vegas that put out a contract on us? And that ended up being confined to a wheelchair? He put a hit out on Miguel and you and us as well to get even for what we did to him."

"Do you think he'll try again?"

Buck put his arm around her shoulder and assured her, "I don't think so. After we talk to the federal judge and explain how he orchestrated a hit from his prison cell I don't think he'll be bothering us anymore."

After making sure Marissa and the kids were okay, Buck went down and rented a rug cleaner to assist in cleaning the red spot off of the rug. The sliding glass window would still need to be replaced but overall everything looked good. Once Buck was finished with shampooing the rug and making sure Marissa and the kids were safe, he headed to the hospital to wait it out with Rachael and Elaine.

Upon arriving at the hospital ER waiting room, Buck walked in to see Elaine and Rachael talking to a doctor. Watching the looks on their faces said a lot about what the doctor's words were to both of them and how it was affecting them. From Elaine's face there was relief that Foster pulled through the operation just fine and was resting comfortably. The prognosis for Foster was not so good for going back to work right away. "The bullet passed through the liver and some of the lower intestines. We were able to patch up the holes left by the bullet, but it will take some time for the healing to take effect," the doctor told them.

By now, Elaine and Rachael were sitting down in the

waiting room.

"How long of a recovery is Foster looking at, doctor?" asked Buck as he walked with the doctor down the corridor.

"About four weeks if everything goes right, maybe six weeks for a worst-case scenario. You should be able to see him in about an hour in his room in the IC unit."

Buck thanked the doctor and went over to where Elaine and Rachael were sitting. After hugging Elaine, he told them where they could find Foster in the IC unit. They all headed in that direction looking for his room. When they reached his room, Foster was already there, still under the effects of the operation. Elaine, taking his hand, kissed it and reached over and whispered in his ear, "I love you; don't you dare die on me now!"

She felt Foster gently squeeze her hand. With tears in her eyes, Elaine smiled, "He's going to be okay."

Buck and Rachael stood there watching with tears in their eyes, holding each other, thankful that Foster was alive and was going to make it.

Buck, leaving the girls, walked outside and looking up into the night sky said, "Thank you for hearing our prayers."

Chapter VIII

Miguel and Lucas walked into the airport in Hermosillo and, looking around, didn't see anything unusual at first. It wasn't until the second sweep that Lucas saw the two men, one was standing at the corner of the counter reading a newspaper and the other man was by the restrooms, nonchalantly reading a book. Pointing this out to Miguel, both of them exited the airport terminal and got back into the truck and left the airport parking lot to continue their drive to Nogales. Having had the airport under surveillance, it was what the two had expected to find.

Lucas called Fernando on his cell phone and found that Fernando was on his way to Nogales, as well. Fernando was able to hitch a ride in an old truck with goats in the back of it. Riding with goats, he got past the checkpoints set up by the cartel people, who were looking for two young men, not an old man riding in the back of a truck.

"Where were the checkpoints at?" Lucas asked Fernando.

"Just outside Hermosillo on the northbound side of the highway."

"Thanks for the update."

Lucas ended the call with Fernando and then updated Miguel about the checkpoints that were up ahead, according to what Fernando had said.

Now Miguel and Lucas were looking for the checkpoint on the road up ahead. Miguel pulled the truck over to the side of the road and asked Lucas, "How do we want to handle the checkpoint?"

"We could blow through the checkpoint or go around it through the desert, or we can ditch the truck and hike the desert again. We have plenty of water to go the distance, if needed."

Miguel considered each one of their options and none of them sounded all that good, except staying with the truck and driving back to Nogales.

"How about we go cross country till we can go no farther and then we hike to Nogales?" Lucas suggested.

"I see that we have no other option, especially if we try to blow our way through the checkpoint. That would create more problems for us, in the long run, than it's worth."

Miguel looked at the gas gauge. "We need to put gas in the truck before we go anywhere."

"I remember seeing a gas station on our way out of town, about a mile back."

They turned the truck around and headed back to the gas station, where they stopped to refuel the truck. Lucas was checking everything in the back of the pickup and came across some boxes of energy bars and another two gallons of water in gallon jugs and a couple boxes of 9mm bullets. Showing Miguel what he had found, he said, "I think we have enough to get us to Nogales, at least, not being thirsty or hungry, and safe, too."

"Actually, this turned out better than I thought it would. We have enough and then some to make it easily to Nogales and to the border."

"I love the way the cartel takes care of its people."

Laughing, Miguel agreed with Lucas and got back into the truck to head out into the desert. One of the men that was sitting and watching at the gas station got on the phone as Miguel and Lucas left. He called the cartel boss to let him know that two gringos were just at the gas station getting gas. The cartel boss said thank you and hung up. Calling the checkpoint on the road, the cartel boss alerted the leader at the roadblock about the red truck coming in his direction.

Miguel turned off the road about a mile down the highway and went about five miles straight out into the desert, away from the road, thinking that this way the dust trail from the truck wouldn't be seen by anybody driving on the highway and wouldn't give away their position as they traveled toward Nogales. Finding an old ATV trail, they followed it until they were about 20 miles into the desert, closer to Nogales. With the sun starting to set, Lucas and Miguel decided to call it a night and camped out, eating their power bars and drinking the water. Lucky for them, the night temperatures were mild, and they didn't need to build a fire to stay warm. A cold camp would be better than being found by somebody seeing the fire.

The leader at the checkpoint, not having seen the red truck pass by, called the cartel boss, "The red truck that the gringos were driving never passed by the checkpoint; what do you want us to do now?"

The cartel boss surmised that the Americans had cut across the desert and ordered his men to search for them in the desert. The leader took his best men and one of the trucks and headed off into the desert to try and find the two Americans, leaving the others to stay put and work the checkpoint, just in case they showed up there anyway.

A little after midnight, Lucas and Miguel were awakened by the sound of a truck engine heading across the desert. Looking from where they were, they could see the headlights of the truck going away from them towards Hermosillo. Miguel looked at Lucas, "We can't stay here any longer; we need to keep moving toward Nogales."

"I agree. How do we plan on doing this at night without being seen by the bad guys?"

"I'll tell you what, I'll walk in front of the truck and you follow me. That way we won't need to have the headlights on."

"Good idea. We'll take turns leading and driving."

With that, Miguel led the way through the desert with Lucas driving with his head out the window, watching Miguel. After about an hour of walking, Miguel changed places with Lucas and proceeded to drive through the desert with Lucas leading the way by foot. The sun was just starting to peek over the mountains in the east, which now made the driving in the desert easier and safer for them, but it also made it easier for them to be seen. Miguel was able to get into the truck with Lucas, and they started to drive faster, now that they could see where they were going. At one point, they stopped for a minute and as Lucas was scanning the area all around them, he saw behind them a cloud of dust being kicked up. He pointed it out to Miguel, and they both knew that the cartel men had found their trail and were in the process of following it to find them.

Miguel and Lucas started driving again, this time looking for a place to hide and hole up till the cartel men lost their trail. Looking for a rock outcropping where their trail would be hard to follow, they kept moving forward. At last, finding a rocky portion of the desert, they turned onto it and made a beeline to a gully where they could conceal themselves. They waited there until the cartel men drove to the rock outcropping. Once the cartel men made it to the outcropping, they lost Miguel and Lucas's trail. The cartel men then stopped their truck and started looking around for the tracks of the truck they were following. Finding none, the cartel men got out to canvass the area, looking for tire tracks in the sand. Eventually tiring of this, the leader called his men back to the truck and they drove forward, hoping to pick up the trail going north.

Miguel and Lucas knew that this cat-and-mouse game had to stop; otherwise, they would never get home. So they decided to follow the cartel men and see if they could stop them somehow. The cartel men searched the desert the entire day looking for Miguel and Lucas, combing every inch of the desert north of them. By nightfall they stopped to set up camp. Miguel and Lucas were waiting for them to do this. After midnight they crept into the camp, and taking the guard out, they went to the truck and pulled all of their supplies and buried them all about a quarter mile from the camp. Before leaving the camp, Miguel crawled under the truck and cut the fuel line to the gas tank in two separate places. He then opened the drain valve on the radiator and let the water drain out.

The next morning when it was still early, Miguel and Lucas drove near the campsite and honked their horn a couple of times and then took off into the desert. The leader, being startled by the arrogance of these two men, ordered his men to get into the truck and chase after Miguel and Lucas. The leader started the truck and drove off with his men to go after the other truck. After about a half mile of chasing them in the desert, the truck stopped and steam was coming out from underneath the hood. When they stopped to see what was wrong with the engine, the leader of the group raised the hood up and found that the engine of the truck was seized and couldn't go any further. By now, one of the men was looking in the bed of the truck and realized that all their food and water was gone. Bringing this to the attention of the leader, the leader started looking for the man who was on guard duty last night but couldn't find him. He put a call out to the cartel boss and explained what had happened to the truck and their supplies. The cartel boss was furious that two men could do so much damage to his business and his soldiers and still slip through their fingers.

Lucas and Miguel made it to Nogales later in the afternoon and were waiting until nightfall to enter the city. Calling Fernando on the phone, Lucas said, "We can see the outskirts of the city. Where are you?"

"I'm, as well, in the outskirts of the city, watching the men patrol up and down the streets in their trucks. I think they are looking for you two guys."

"No doubt, the cartel boss can't afford to let us get to the American side."

"Tell Fernando we'll be in there tonight after dark. Where does he want to meet us?" Miguel asked.

"There is a cantina called Dew Drop Inn. It's located in the southeastern part of the city, about three blocks in from the edge of town. I will wait for you there."

Miguel and Lucas knew it wouldn't be long before the

cartel men that they had left in the desert would be looking for them again. So they drove until they found a well-traveled road that led to the city from the south end. They parked their truck just inside the city and waited for darkness to come. Fernando was right; the cartel boss had his men driving through the streets trying to locate the two men who had his hard drives. After counting the times the cartel men drove through the area, Miguel noticed a pattern to the patrols. It seemed the patrol would come by approximately every 30 minutes in this area. Knowing this, Miguel figured they had 30 minutes to get to Fernando and pick him up and head to the border station. Once there at the station, they would be safe. At about seven-thirty pm they started into the city, looking for the cantina where Fernando would be. Leaving right after the patrol had made their sweep through the area, they followed behind the patrol to find Fernando. At about eight o'clock they found the Dew Drop Inn cantina and, parking the truck behind the building, Miguel walked into the cantina through the back door. Lucas stayed outside, watching the street for any sign of the patrols.

After Miguel walked into the back of the cantina, staying in the shadows, he saw Fernando sitting in the middle of the room with two guards standing over him. Miguel could see that he had been beat up and was bleeding from his nose. There was a third man sitting at one of the tables, who was the boss of the two men guarding Fernando. Miguel stood there for a minute, scanning the room to see if there were any more men in there that worked for the cartel. Seeing none, he headed out the back door and told Lucas, "Fernando has got himself captured and is being watched by at least three men in the center of the cantina."

"And the fun just keeps coming our way."

"We need to create a distraction that will draw them away from Fernando so one of us can get him out of there. Any ideas on how we do that?"

Lucas thought for a moment. "I think I've an idea on what to do." Lucas continued, "I will start a fire out front on the porch, and you come in the back and grab Fernando and bring him back here. Then we'll drive out of here to the border."

"You know, you keep this up and you might get promoted and be able to have a decent job someday, like working for the police department. If you're lucky, I'll even put in a good word for you," said Miguel, smiling.

"I'm not worthy," Lucas said, returning the smile. As Lucas left and headed to the front of the cantina, Miguel made his way to the back door of the cantina again.

About five minutes later, the owner of the cantina could smell smoke and yelled fire. The boss and the owner went to the front of the cantina and saw the fire burning at the front entrance of the place. By now, the boss was calling for one of the guards to help put out the fire. The front of the cantina, being built of dry wood, caught fire, which started to spread out of control. Miguel walked into the cantina, shot the one guard, and grabbed Fernando. He then half-carried him through the back door, and then they made their way to where the truck was located.

The boss, seeing that his man was down and that Fernando was gone, headed to the back of the cantina, looking for Fernando. Lucas, after starting the fire, went to the back of the cantina to provide cover for Miguel and Fernando to leave. The boss and the other guard stepped outside the cantina, looking for Fernando. Lucas fired his gun twice and both men went down. The boss was only wounded and was trying to get back inside the cantina, which by now was totally engulfed in flames. With nowhere to go, the boss lay there on the ground, not being able to move. Lucas came over to where the boss was lying on the ground and looked at him. "Does it hurt being shot like that?"

The boss asked Lucas to help him. "I'll give you money if you help me."

Lucas, looking at him and seeing the wound in his chest and knowing it would be only minutes before he died, said, "Your money is no good to me."

As he walked away, the boss continued to plead for his life by offering Lucas more money. In a few minutes the boss quit talking and was dead.

Lucas made his way to where the truck was parked and, seeing Fernando and Miguel waiting there, got into the truck.   Miguel then drove to the border station which separated Mexico and the U.S.

Lucas looked behind him and saw the smoke billowing into the night sky and smiled, thinking to himself, *"One less place for the cartel to call home in Nogales."*   Reaching the border, the personnel at the station asked if they had anything to declare before entering the U.S., and Lucas said, after showing their ID cards, "I'd like to declare we are Americans and are very glad to be back in the USA."

The guard smiled at them. "Welcome home."

Chapter VIX

Agent Smith was in the Nogales Border Patrol building, waiting for Miguel, Lucas, and Fernando to show up in the office. Having all three back and in one piece was excellent work on their part and mighty good luck on Smith's part. Smith had a stenographer to record and copy down the initial report of events as they each told their parts.

Miguel went first, and as the others listened to him speak, they confirmed or kept silent. When it was Lucas's turn, he told about removing the hard drives from the computers and giving them to Miguel for safekeeping. At this point, Lucas said to Miguel, "You might want to give them to him now."

Smith interrupted, "We already got them about a day ago."

"What do you mean you already got them?" asked Lucas.

Miguel interjected, "I sent them through the mail, actually FedEx, before we left the Culiacan airport."

"When did you do that?" asked Lucas.

"Remember when I was late getting back to the truck and you guys were getting nervous? The reason was is that I figured it would be easier to ship them than to carry them and maybe get caught with them on us. So I sent them by FedEx and knew they would get there, even if we didn't."

Fernando was smiling, as was Smith, when Lucas put all the pieces together and just sat there for a moment. Then Lucas looked up at Miguel, smiling, "Man, you can't trust any of these Phoenix cops for nothing, can you? In all actuality, it was a pretty good idea at that. The fact is, I wish I would have thought of it myself."

Smith, still smiling, said, "The information on the hard drives is giving us good Intel about the cartel boss's network. And, as we speak, we are arresting people who are on the payroll in our security setup. In fact, some of them have already crossed the border back into Mexico and are being rounded up by the Mexican police to be brought back to the United States to face charges and trials."

After the briefings were over, Smith pulled Miguel aside and started to talk to him privately. "First of all, your family is okay."

This caught Miguel's attention right off the bat. "What do you mean, my family is okay?"

"Well, there was this incident at your home dealing with a couple of hit men trying to kill you and your family. This happened while you were under cover in Mexico. Fortunately, we got there in time to stop the hit on your wife and kids; it was a combined effort by the FBI, state police, and your parents. Both of the hit men are dead, and we're trying find out who ordered the hit so it doesn't happen again."

After listening to Smith, Miguel asked, "Can I call home and talk to my wife, Marissa?"

"Of course, you can," said Smith.

When Miguel asked to be excused to make the call, Smith left the room and left Miguel alone in the office. Miguel dialed his home number and let it ring a couple of times before Marissa answered the phone.

"I'm back and I'm safe, how about you?" Miguel asked.

"I'm safe and so are the kids. When are you coming home?"

"I'll be home tonight with any luck to tuck the kids in bed. I heard you had some fun with the in-laws at the house?"

"Well, it was quite interesting, to say the least; I'll tell you all about it when you get home tonight."

"Are you all right?"

"Now that I know you're safe, I am. I love you and miss you."

"I love you and miss you, too. Have I got a story for you, as well. Well, I better get going if I'm to be home tonight."

"Hurry home and drive safe. Goodbye."

"I will, and goodbye."

Miguel walked out of the office and headed to where Lucas and Fernando were in the cafeteria eating. Lucas looked up, "Everything all right at home?"

Miguel nodded. "It is, now that I called."

"Well, I don't know about you, but I feel like we earned some time off for at least a day or two, anyway, and I know just the person I want to spend some time with."

"It wouldn't be Amanda who works the soup kitchen, would it?" asked Miguel.

"Why, how did you know that? Man, I'm telling you these guys from Phoenix are really sharp nowadays," Lucas replied, laughing.

"Have you called her yet?" asked Smith as he came walking up to the group.

"As a matter of fact, I have, and we have a date for tomorrow after she's done at work, to go to a fancy restaurant like Burger King or something like that."

Fernando laughed, "You gringos sure know how to impress the senoritas."

"I owe it all to my parents; they taught me everything I know. Besides, it worked on my mom when my dad started dating her," Lucas said, laughing.

"I have got to meet your parents," said Smith.

"Me too," said Miguel and Fernando at the same time.

They all laughed and sat there eating, after a while, Lucas said, "Well, I need to get going and get cleaned up. The way I look, it could take till tomorrow to get it done. I'll see you guys in a couple of days, all right?"

Smith and Miguel both said, "Goodbye, and good luck on your date with Amanda. I'm sure it will be unforgettable for her."

Fernando went with Lucas to head back to the soup kitchen and some well-deserved rest. Miguel sat there eating his sandwich, with Smith drinking some coffee. Smith got up first. "Whenever you're ready to leave, let me know. I'll drive you up to Phoenix and drop you off at the office to pick up your car."

Miguel wolfed down his sandwich. "I'm ready now if you are."

"Let's go, then."

On the way back to Phoenix Miguel slept most the time. Arriving in Phoenix at the federal building, Miguel jumped into his car and headed home to Glendale. Upon getting home, the kids came running out to meet their daddy, and Marissa was following close behind. After giving each of the kids a hug and a kiss, he stood up and gave Marissa a hug and a long kiss. The kids were jumping and making noises all around their daddy while he walked arm in arm with the first love of his life. Closing the door and tuning out the world, everything was right inside the world of Miguel and Marissa.

Lucas got home just in time to clean up and meet Amanda for a surprise get together. Hoping to take her out to dinner, he ended up working at the soup kitchen for the rest of the evening with her. He didn't mind at all, as long as he was with her. Watching her laugh and joke with the people she was helping as they came through the line for food and drink made Lucas wonder where she had been all his life. Every once in a while, he would catch her eye and she would smile at him and he would smile back. He had never felt this way about anybody else he had known in his life. With Amanda around, he wanted to treasure her and protect her from the bad things in the world. Lucas was truly in love with her, and in only a short time he knew he wanted to spend the rest of his life with her. He could tell that she liked him, as well, and the next few days would go by too fast and would end too soon for him. In the meantime, he would have to make the most of their time together.

Chapter X

When the two days were over, both Miguel and Lucas were sitting at their desks and talking about what they had done with their days off. They both seemed to have recovered from their experience in the deserts of Mexico. Smith came in with a round of coffee for each of them, and as they sat there talking about being back in the real world, he opened a folder and handed to them the printed information they were able to glean from the hard drives. Over the next three hours, using maps, highlighters, and stick pins, they mapped out all the locations for the cartel contacts on both sides of the border. Once that was completed, they prioritized the list of names and places for the Mexican police and the local law enforcement organizations to conduct their raids. The question that kept coming up was, who would go after the people that worked for the cartel. To Lucas and Miguel, it wasn't about the credit, it was about the logistics and how to pick the people up without alarming the others. This process of identifying the people and picking them up took a week for them to line everything up just right.

During this time of racking and stacking names and locations, Miguel came across a name he remembered from his first outing with the Border Patrol. It seems that a certain Captain Diego Montoya was on the payroll of the cartel, usually handling the mules and human-trafficking part of the operation. Seeing this, Miguel walked over to Lucas's desk and laid out the information he had, pointing to Captain Diego Montoya's name. After studying it for a moment, Lucas's eyes got big and a smile crossed his face. He looked up at Miguel, who was smiling as well, and nodded. Both of them walked over to Smith's desk and laid the paperwork out for him to see. Smith studied it for a minute and a smile came to his face, and looking at both of them, he asked, "So, I take it you want to go after the captain, do you?"

"Gee, boss, I didn't think you would ever ask," Lucas said with a big Cheshire cat grin on his face.

Miguel, with a smile of anticipation on his face, asked, "When can we leave to go get him?"

Smith looked at both of them, "I guess saying no is out of the question, isn't it? We need to let the Mexican police handle his arrest. That being said, if you were able to assist them in this endeavor, I'm sure they would really appreciate your help."

Both Miguel and Lucas were already thinking about where they would have to go to find the captain. Smith broke their train of thought, "I need you to give me a profile on the captain and his operation so I can get permission for our part in this. I suspect he isn't operating on his own, and we need to know how large his network is and who else is involved on both sides of the border."

Both Miguel and Lucas started combing through the materials and identifying locations and other people involved in the human and drug-trafficking operations going on in that part of Mexico. They found that Yuma was the closest big city in the United States that could be reached using State Route 95 from the border. The city was ideal for human trafficking and drug running, which spread from there into other cities and states.

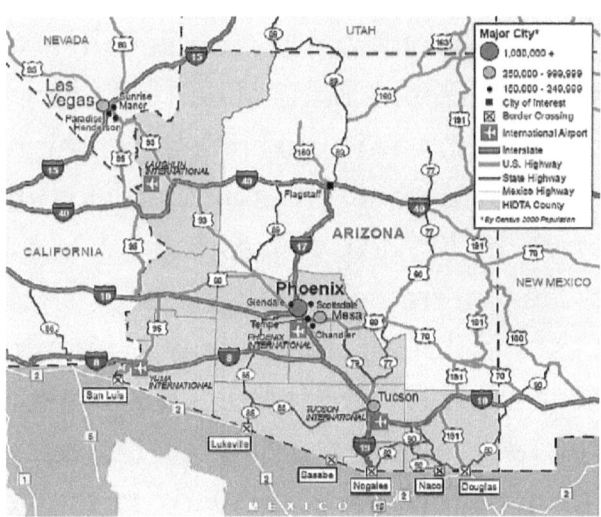

This Infrastructure was provided by the National Drug Intel Center.

With the new information derived from the hard drives, they built a map showing the traffic routes through Arizona, which showed the areas of High Intensity Drug Traffic Areas (HIDTA).

The Arizona HIDTA region encompasses the western and southern counties of Cochise, La Paz, Maricopa, Mohave, Pima, Pinal, Santa Cruz, and Yuma and includes the entire U.S.-Mexico border in Arizona. The HIDTA region also contains a number of federal lands controlled by the U.S. Department of Defense, U.S. Forest Service, National Park Service, and Bureau of Indian Affairs. The proximity to the U.S.-Mexico border itself, with a remote, largely under-protected border area between Arizona's ports of entry (POEs), combined with access to infrastructure such as the highways that connect major Arizona cities with major illicit drug-source areas in Mexico, makes the HIDTA region an attractive area for traffickers.

While 323 miles of the 376-mile Arizona–Mexico border have some type of fencing, few physical barriers exist elsewhere along the border between POEs to impede drug traffickers, particularly in the West Desert area of the U.S. Border Patrol (USBP) Tucson Sector. In addition, traffickers are able to easily conceal drug shipments among the high volume of legitimate cross-border traffic at the region's POEs, creating significant challenges for law-enforcement officers. Thousands of private vehicles, commercial tractor-trailers, and pedestrians that cross the U.S.–Mexico border daily provide ideal cover for drug and bulk-cash smuggling operations.

The Arizona HIDTA region's position along the U.S.–Mexico border also makes it an attractive location for other illicit operations. Drug traffickers and other criminal groups engage in activities such as firearms trafficking and alien smuggling. Alien smuggling is a growing concern to law-enforcement officials in the Arizona HIDTA region. Criminal organizations smuggle aliens, some of whom are members of gangs such as Mara Salvatrucha (MS 13), into the United States. These individuals typically have extensive criminal records and pose a threat, not only to the Arizona HIDTA region, but also to communities throughout the United States. (This was provided by the National Drug Intel Center.)

With the map complete, Lucas and Miguel concentrated on the area around Yuma and its corridor of human trafficking, as well as the drug trade. The biggest kind of drug coming into the U.S. was methamphetamine, created in Mexico and shipped across the border, with marijuana being the next biggest drug coming across. Miguel and Lucas were surprised to find the cartel had people in scuba gear carrying their bundles of drugs through the sewer system in Douglas, Arizona.

By now, Smith had enough information to go to his

bosses and justify sending Miguel and Lucas back across the border into Mexico to go after Captain Montoya and disrupt his operation. After a couple of hours in the meeting, Smith came back to his office and sat down, while Miguel and Lucas waited to hear the results of the meeting. Smith got up to grab a cup of coffee and as he went back to his office, he sat down again. By now, Lucas couldn't take it anymore. "Well, what did they say?"

Smith looked up with a frown on his face. "It's a go for you two."

Lucas looked at him. "Man, you're killing me."

Miguel nodded in agreement. "That was pretty mean, boss."

"It was all I could do not to laugh at you two being so eager to go," Smith said, smiling.

At that point, Lucas and Miguel proceeded to prepare for their trip back into Mexico and to meet their nemesis, Captain Montoya, and the others he had under his control. This would mean going back to the part of the desert where they encountered the captain that one time at the river crossing.

Smith told them to be ready in two days and he would have the Border Patrol bring them to the same spot as before. There would be a meeting with the Border Patrol supervisors and Smith's team before they left to go. The meeting was scheduled the same day as their departure into Mexico.

Miguel went home to see Marissa to let her know that he would be going back into Mexico and that it should only be a couple of days and he'd be back home. Lucas drove to Nogales to say his goodbyes to Amanda before leaving. They had a date that night and from there he drove to Yuma to the Federal building. Miguel and Lucas met Smith in Yuma and they drove together to San Louis. The others at meeting were waiting for the three of them to get there. Once seated, the first thing the speaker said as he introduced Lucas and Miguel was, "These guys are the ones that stole and delivered the hard drives from the cartel boss in Mexico."

The others in the group stood up and clapped to show their appreciation for their accomplishment. As far as the Border Patrol was concerned, having the information made available to them cut their time in half, when it came to knowing where the bad guys would show up and catching them red-handed with the drugs, weapons, and people.

After the introduction, the meeting began with a power-point slide presentation, showing the call signs and passwords to be used in case any problems arose. A map was shown, giving the location of the captain, plus a list of known bad guys, with pictures, known to frequent the area and the towns they supposedly lived in. Each name and picture had a brief rap sheet as to why they were wanted by the Mexican police.

One of the conditions for the trip was that they would

have support from the Mexican Federal Police in order to arrest anybody on their side of the border. The speaker introduced Jose Louis as their counterpart from Mexico. Jose stood up and waved at everybody in the room. The speaker listed off the pertinent information about Jose. He had been on the force for over ten years and had worked in the drug unit for the last five years. He had been trained by the DEA and the Border Patrol in their procedures to combat the drug problems and had been given a refresher course in human trafficking. He was married and had five children and was considered to be above reproach as to his integrity.

Jose did part of the briefing from the Mexican perspective. He started his portion of the brief with a picture of Captain Montoya and his first sergeant. He stated, "The captain has been under investigation for accepting bribes and kickbacks from the cartel for years. Just when they had him, the witness would come up missing or recant his story to stay alive. The sergeant is no better. His name is Hector Sanchez. He is considered to be the henchman for the captain's dirty work." Jose clicked on the next slide. "His soldiers were handpicked for their disregard for rules and regulations; basically, a gang wearing uniforms for their own purposes."

Lucas looked at Miguel, "Thanks for not letting me get shot that day. I didn't realize who we were dealing with."

Miguel looked at him, "I've seen these kinds of soldiers all over my hometown in Colombia. That's how I knew what they would do to you if given half a chance."

When the briefing was over, Smith motioned for Miguel and Lucas to meet with the Border Patrol Chief and sit and talk to him for a moment. The chief shook both of their hands and offered a seat to them. The chief spoke first, "We want this captain really bad and any others that you find out there. That being said, you watch your back at all times out there. Jose is good people, but that doesn't mean anything when you are out there by yourselves."

Smith nodded, "The enemy of my enemy is my friend, but in the end, he is still my enemy. You know what I'm getting at?"

Miguel and Lucas looked at both of them and nodded their heads. "In other words, we're on our own out there," Miguel said.

The chief nodded, and Smith said, "That you are, my friends."

Chapter XI

As Buck and Rachael left the hospital after visiting Foster again, both of them seemed to be in a good mood since Foster had first been shot. The doctors were all impressed with how fast he was healing. He was getting bored sitting in the hospital and raising hell over the food they were making him eat. In fact, he asked Buck to order him a pizza and sneak it in for him; however, when Elaine heard about it, she put her foot down really quick. "If you do, he won't take you fishing on his boat when he gets out of here."

Buck took that as the gospel according to Elaine and begged for forgiveness for thinking about it for even a second.

Foster was getting better and would soon be able to show his scar to his comrades in arms. All kidding aside, Buck and Rachael were thankful that he was okay. Earlier in the day, Buck had placed a call to Evans to let him know what had happened to Foster and how close it had been for Marissa and his godchildren. Evans was upset by the attempted hit and asked Buck, "What do you want me to do from here?"

"I need to know who authorized the hit. It had to have come from somebody higher than Frankie," Buck replied.

"Let me look into it and see what I can find out for you."

Buck and Rachael, realizing that everything was good for all involved, decided to head back to Smith County to carry on with the duties and jobs they had waiting for them. They decided to stop first at Miguel and Marissa's house to see the kids and Marissa one more time before leaving.

The kids were upset and wanted to go with them, as usual, but once they understood that they couldn't go, they were promised that they could go see Grandma and Grandpa in the wintertime during Christmas. Marissa was the most upset by them leaving to go back. The attempted hit was something that you read about or happens to someone else, not this close or to yourself. After some crying and hugging by all involved, Buck and Rachael were finally able to leave, with a promise that they would be there quickly if something else should occur. Marissa was strong, but it was the thought of her children being hurt that caused such concern. She wouldn't know how to handle it if the children were hurt in any way. Buck and Rachael understood this with their own children, as well, and were just as protective towards them.

On the drive back to Smith County Buck told Rachael about the phone call to Evans in Las Vegas.

"What did he have to say about all of this?" Rachael

asked.

"He said that he was going to look into it some more to find out who authorized the hit and that he would let us know if anything turned up."

"That's good to know. What do you want to do when you find out who did it?"

"I don't know right offhand, but I think a visit from us would be appropriate, don't you?"

"I agree that we should pay our respects to them. It's the least we can do to show our appreciation to them."

"I agree; besides, I have something I want to give back to them."

With that, they drove home in silence back to Smith County, looking forward to seeing the kids and getting back to work. Arriving late in the evening and not wanting to awaken the children, they thought it best to wait till tomorrow to pick them up. As they unloaded the truck, taking their suitcases in with them, the house seemed strangely quiet with no kids running around, almost as if it was empty of life. Buck reached for Rachael and, holding her, he whispered into her ear, "You know the kids are gone and we're alone, just like it used to be."

Rachael smiled, "You want to pretend we're dating again?"

"Sounds good to me."

"In that case, I need to be home before my midnight curfew, and my parents are not the least understanding if I'm late coming home."

"Does that mean that it's time to take you home now?"

Rachael nodded., "Besides, I'm not that kind of girl, anyway."

"Oh sure, I fall in love with a nun. Talk about luck," Buck said, kissing her.

Rachael replied, giggling, "But I'll tell you that my parents are gone for the weekend, and they'll never know unless you tell them."

"My lips are sealed."

And with that, the lights went out and the suitcases would be taken care of tomorrow.

The next morning coming into work, the paperwork was stacked high on Buck's desk, waiting to be reviewed and signed or handled accordingly. Buck sat down with his first cup of coffee and listened to his secretary talk about all the meetings and appointments that had to be reset for when he was gone. Sitting there, he now was starting to understand how being a lowly deputy wasn't such a bad place to be in life, no meetings, no politics, and no deadlines to meet.

Rachael came in and saw the overwhelmed look on his face and started to help with the paperwork and rescheduling the meetings for him. After about an hour, they were able to make heads and tails of the backlog of work. That being done, Rachael headed out the door to go get the kids from Dave and Linda, who had been watching them at their house. Arriving at the house, the kids were excited to see their mom again and were excited to be going home. Rachael gave the kids a great big hug from both of the parents. Because their dad was at work, the hug from mom would have to do until he got home.

For Rachael and Buck, things were back to normal and they were thankful for it. The world seemed to be going in the right direction with no surprises for them, although it would take them several days to get fully acclimated into their normal routine again, with each of them wanting to go back out and play cops and robbers instead of staying and doing paperwork.

Chapter XII

After the closed-door meeting was over between the chief and Agent Smith, Miguel and Lucas, escorted by the chief, headed out the door to get into one of the Ford six-pack pickups that the Border Patrol used. "I wish you luck and good hunting," said Smith.

Miguel and Lucas, along with Jose, who was already seated in the front seat of the pickup waiting for them to get in, said, "Thanks."

A Border Patrol agent named Davis got into the driver's seat, "Any you guys want to pick up anything before we head out into the desert?"

"I would like to pick up a slushy before we head out," Lucas said.

"I would like to get bananas myself," said Miguel.

Jose, thinking about it, said, "I would like to pick up some candy bars."

So Davis took them to the local gas station to get what they wanted before leaving for the desert. Being quite content with their food, they headed into the desert, where they had come across Captain Montoya at the river. Davis dropped them off at that spot, and they said their goodbyes and good lucks.

Their mission was to catch Captain Montoya and

his men in the act of human and drug trafficking, either in pictures or red-handed. The goal was to have proof of his involvement in either or both of these crimes, then turn it over to the Mexican government for action. The problem was making sure that the Mexican government was going to do something about it.

They stood there watching Davis drive away, and after a minute or two of checking their gear, they started following the trail left by the 2.5-ton trucks that belonged to captain Montoya. At times, it was hard to follow the tracks of the trucks due to weather conditions changing the trail, but they had an idea of where they were heading. Occasionally, they would find an unmarked grave along the way, next to the trail. Miguel and Lucas knew these were some of the people that the captain had taken back with him that didn't make it. Both Miguel and Lucas knew that their deaths didn't have to be, but there was no use arguing about it; the captain would eventually have to answer for these deaths, as well. After about three hours of hiking, they stood on the hill overlooking the base of operations for Captain Montoya and his men. The base itself wasn't all that big, just a group of buildings in the middle of a small dry lake bed. There was some brush located on the south end of the base. The fence around the base provided some sense of security, although some of it was in disrepair. The buildings were located in the center of the compound, and everything else, like the trucks and jeeps, was spread out around the perimeter. The center building looked like it was the captain's headquarters, this being where the flagpole with the flag of Mexico was raised.

From their perch, they could see the day-to-day activities of the base, and with telephoto lenses on the cameras they could get close-up pictures of everything going on. The biggest issue for the team was being caught by an unknown player happening to stumble upon their camp. During the days, the three of them could hide in the brush without being seen. At night, they could get closer to the base and listen in on the conversations of the soldiers in the camp. They accomplished this with two of them at a time going down. One person would provide security while the other person would reconnoiter the area, and both would come back before dawn to sleep and brief the third man on what they had learned. They would transmit all information that was important to the Border Patrol radio communications room with the updates.

After getting their camp situated and the communications equipment checked out, they drew straws for the first night of collecting Intel. Lucas and Jose drew the short straws and prepared themselves to go. Miguel would sit and watch from above, and with earwigs he would be in communication to help keep an eye on any new developments.

Their camp was such that the team couldn't afford to go the same way up and down the mountain; otherwise, someone would possibly see the trail and get curious as to where it went. Each time they went down they would have to find a different way to get there. Tonight would be the easiest for the team; they could go directly to the base and find another way back. Lucas and Jose started down the hill about seven o'clock pm, walking and stopping every so often to listen and watch for anything unusual, then proceeded another 10 or 20 feet and stop again. The base was approximately half-a-mile away and getting there took some time just to be safe. About nine o'clock they were in position by the fence line surrounding the base. Looking for a spot in the fence they could cut into without somebody finding it later was their next task. Once this was done, this opening in the fence would be their proverbial door to the base. Lucas and Jose found a spot behind some old trucks that were abandoned and were rusting in the desert. The trucks provided cover in and out of the base without being seen by anyone.

Once inside the base, they verified the maps that they had drawn, using their telephoto lenses as to what each building was. The goal was to be where the talk was loose and fast and, if need be, use their communication equipment for their own purposes. Once the layout of the camp was verified, Lucas and Jose went about checking the camp for a jail, not only to find prisoners but also to find a place where they could lay low inside the base, if need be. With all the logistics squared away, the Intel collection could begin. Jose would lead off and Lucas would follow and provide cover and an extra set of ears, if needed. They went from building to building, sitting under the open windows listening to what was being said. If nothing of value was picked up, they would move on to the next window. This went on for the rest of the evening, going from window to window until they got to the communications building. There they sat under the window, listening to the radioman talking on the radio, with one other soldier inside. From their conversation, something was going to happen in a couple of days and Captain Montoya was to be part of it. The problem was, neither Jose nor Lucas could determine if it was official or from someone else. Writing everything down on paper so as not to forget anything, Lucas and Jose stayed there until four o'clock in the morning before deciding to leave the base. Making their way back to the old truck area, they crossed through the fence and made their way back using an alternate route to their camp. Arriving at about six o'clock, they let Miguel know what was going on and then sent a message to the Border Patrol base radio communications center. At that point, both Lucas and Jose went to sleep while Miguel kept guard.

That night it was Miguel's turn to go to the base. Again drawing straws, Jose was the one picked to go with him. As they geared up to go, Jose sat there eating the last candy bar he had, and afterwards said, "Gentlemen, I think it is time to go; I have finished my last candy bar and there are none left. We are at a crisis with no candy bars; I'm not sure I can go on."

All of them laughed at the comment, "Maybe they have a candy machine at the base where we can get you some more," Miguel said.

"That is a good idea, my friend." said Jose.

"Here you go. I was saving this for later, but if it will save the mission, you may have it," Lucas replied, smiling.

"I'm not worthy of such friends as you," Jose said as he grabbed the candy bar from Lucas.

With his candy bar in Jose's pocket and the gear ready to go, Miguel and Jose headed down the hill toward the back of the base to reconnoiter the area again. After clearing the fence into the base, they made their way back to the communications building and sat there, listening to the radio operator inside talk back and forth on the radio. Miguel and Jose knew from the night before that something was going to happen in the next couple of days. What it was, they couldn't tell for sure. Now, as they listened to the radio operator, they learned of another group of migrants coming up from the south to cross the river as the last group had tried to before. Again, not being able to tell if the report was official or not, they would have to wait and see.

After finding that the base had settled down for the evening, Jose and Miguel went from building to building, listening to the conversations from the soldiers inside, most of which concerned their loved ones and when they would be able to be with them again. Going over to where the captain's quarters were, they sat and listened for any conversation coming from the captain. This night, the captain got a call on his cell phone from somebody important; they could tell this by the tone in the captain's voice. As Miguel and Jose sat and listened to the conversation, the captain was giving out information on an exercise he planned on doing tomorrow near the river with his men. After the captain ended his phone call, he called for the sergeant to report to him immediately. A young soldier went out to look for the sergeant to bring him back. After about five minutes, the sergeant appeared, "You sent for me, Captain?"

"Yes, we have a mission to perform tomorrow, Sergeant. I need the men ready to go early in the morning. It seems we have some people trying to cross the border into America, and we need to stop them from getting there."

"How do you want us to handle this, Captain?"

"The same way as before. These people do not have permission from our boss to cross over, and they will be carrying drugs and anything that they think is necessary to take into America. We need to get the drugs and anything else of value and get rid of them permanently, do you understand, Sergeant?"

The sergeant saluted. "All will be ready tomorrow, Captain."

"Good, see to it, Sergeant."

At this point, having heard the captain's plan for tomorrow, Jose and Miguel headed back to their own camp. Reaching the camp at midnight, they told Lucas of the captain's plan for tomorrow morning. Lucas, using the satphone, got hold of the Border Patrol office communications center and let them know what was about to happen. The Border Patrol office acknowledged the message and let Lucas know they would be in touch with them.

Waiting for the return phone call, Miguel sat there, wondering if there was something they could do to stop the captain before he left the base. After a minute, Miguel said, thinking out loud, "What would happen if they couldn't support the drug runners or the traffickers?"

"He would be in deep doo-doo, wouldn't he," Lucas replied.

Jose looked at both of them and smiled. "Are you saying we could stop him before he got started?"

Miguel and Lucas nodded their heads in unison.

"How do we do that?" asked Jose.

Lucas spoke first, "We could sabotage the trucks while they're at the base."

"I like what you're thinking. We stop him before he starts and we nail the mules and traffickers on this side of the border before they cross over the river," Jose said, excitedly.

"If we do it, we need to do it now, under the cover of darkness. This is your call, Jose; what do you want to do?" Miguel asked.

Jose looked at his watch, knowing it was at least 30 minutes, maybe 45 minutes, back to the base. "It's one-thirty; we need to go now if we go."

Lucas was gathering his gear to go and Miguel was picking up his gear, as well, waiting for Jose to make a decision. As Jose watched the two of them getting ready, he looked at Lucas and Miguel, "Do you think they have a candy machine down there at the base?"

"If we can find one, I'll buy you a candy bar," Lucas said as he started back down the mountain.

Miguel and Jose followed closely behind him, with Jose saying, "You promise about the candy bar, Lucas?"

Entering the base again, they found the trucks that would be used the next day, parked in front of the captain's quarters. Lucas and Miguel knew sabotaging the trucks couldn't be obvious. The trucks had to look normal at first appearance to the trained eye. Not knowing beforehand what they were going to do, they sat at the fence line and debated what they could do to stop the trucks. Giving it some thought, Miguel came up with the idea of messing with the fuel lines on the trucks.

"What can we use to do that?" Lucas asked.

"I know just the place to go; follow me," Jose said. Lucas and Miguel followed Jose to the chow hall and, getting to the back door, Lucas jimmied it open for them. Looking around inside the kitchen area, Jose found some pound bags of sugar. Grabbing all they could carry, they headed out the same door they had come in. Before leaving the kitchen, Miguel and Lucas stood there looking at the salt bags lined up in a row. Grabbing about six bags of salt, they closed the door and followed Jose. Catching up with Jose, they found him pouring the sugar into the gas tanks in each truck, making sure there wasn't any hint of the sugar anywhere near the fuel tanks. Once this was done, Lucas pointed to the water tank for the base and then pointed at the salt, smiling. Jose nodded his head and all three of them headed to the water tank. Climbing up the ladder to the opening of the water tank, they poured the salt into the water and then quickly climbed down the ladder. As they made their way back to the opening in the fence, they could see the rays of the sun starting to light up the sky in the east.

Later that morning, all three of them were watching the base camp from their perch as it came to life to start a new day. The trucks were turned over to get the engines warmed up for the trip, and the men were eating their breakfast in the chow hall. All three of them were chuckling about what they had done earlier in the night. They could see the cook taking the containers of milk out the back and throwing the milk away. And as they sat there watching the camp, the engine on one of the trucks sputtered and died. They could see the mechanics raise the hood on the truck, trying to figure out why it quit running. Pretty soon, the second truck quit running as well. The captain was outside looking at the mechanic, yelling at him to fix the trucks. The mechanic called the others over to help with the trucks. By now, all of the trucks were dead and wouldn't start. Captain Montoya was totally out of control, yelling at the mechanics to do something about the trucks. One of the sergeants came over and started talking to the captain about some of the men being sick and not knowing why. Jose was reading the sergeant's lips, and in between laughing, he told Miguel and Lucas what he was saying. By now, all three of the guys were rolling on the ground, laughing at the hysterics going on down on the base.

The satphone rang as the team watched the theatrics down below; it was the Border Patrol chief on the line, asking if there were more updates for him. In between the laughs, Miguel explained what they had done and that the captain wasn't going anywhere this morning. The chief, sitting in his office, just listened to Miguel as he told him what was happening below at the base. The chief smiled, "I need you guys to get down to the river just in case the bad guys still find a way to get there."

"Yes, sir. We are on our way now."

The chief was laughing when he hung up the phone and Smith, who was sitting there, looked at him. "What's so funny, Chief?"

The chief proceeded to tell Smith what his guys had done and that the captain was going to be late, if he made it at all, to the river. Smith just shook his head and smiled. "I wonder if what they've done will cause an international incident?" he said as he got ready to go with the chief to the river.

Captain Montoya was adamant about having his men get to the river on time. Finding any kind of vehicle to take, they loaded up the men who were able to make the trip and headed off into the desert. With the captain in his jeep and his men following in cars and small pickups, they made a single-file line going through the desert. From a distance, they looked like ants marching one behind the other.

Having to hike to the river to meet the captain and his men, Jose, Miguel and Lucas had to run to make it in time. Jose was paying for all the candy bars he had bought and borrowed from Lucas. Miguel and Lucas placed themselves along the opening of the valley, waiting for the captain and his army to show. Jose made his way closer to the river, hoping to see firsthand all that was about to unfold, just in case they needed an eyewitness. As Lucas and Miguel sat and started to breathe more normally, Lucas signaled Miguel that he could see the illegals coming up the valley just ahead of the captain and his men. Miguel waved at Lucas to acknowledge his message and moved behind the rocks to be out of sight of the illegals as they made their way to the river. Lucas was in a better spot; he was behind the rocks on the other side and was able to see more clearly what was coming in and out of the chokepoint.

Lucas, looking below, saw some men come from one of the side canyons and start lining up on his side of the rocks. Each of them had a rifle and handgun. Lucas tried to signal Miguel about the men below him, but he wasn't sure that Miguel had seen his signal, while, in fact, Miguel saw the men before Lucas had. Miguel moved from his spot and got closer to the valley floor and waited for the illegals to come through. Lucas, seeing Miguel move, got closer to the men below him and was waiting for the illegals to come through. Jose was just now starting to see the illegals moving through the chokepoint. The group was comprised of illegals being trafficked and others that were carrying bundles on their backs. The guards were carrying rifles and forcing the ones carrying the bundles to keep moving towards the river. Jose, realizing that he had no protection from the view of the guerillas where he was at, ended up moving to the other side of the river onto American soil and repositioning himself behind a rock outcropping, where he waited.

Up on the ridge, overlooking the river on the American side, the Border Patrol was in place with cameras and rifles to keep the illegals from coming onto the American side of the river. The chief and Smith were part of the crew watching the valley below. The guards in the group of illegals were very nervous and extremely cautious about this part of the hike since, the last time, the Mexican Army showed up and took the drugs and the illegals back to Mexico. Moving in and through the rocks to give them some protection from whoever was out there, the guards pushed the illegals forward to the river.

The first shot rang out, dropping one of the two guards in his tracks. The second guard hid behind some rocks and tried to see where the shot had come from. Firing into the area where he thought the shot originated from, he rose up to fire. As he did this, one of the guerrillas fired his rifle and hit him in the head, killing him instantly. With the second guard down, there was no protection for the illegals. Making a run for the river, the illegals started to cross the river, when the guerrillas came out from behind the rocks and started firing into the group.

Lucas and Miguel, seeing what was about to happen, started firing into the guerrillas to stop them. Two of the guerillas dropped as they were moving forward toward the illegals. At first, the guerillas didn't realize they had lost two men and, when they did, they were confused as to who and where the firing was coming from. Stopping in their tracks, they stood there looking for Miguel and Lucas. By then, two more men fell dead; and with only six men left, they took off into the rocks in front of Lucas, hoping to hide there. Lucas continued to fire into the group, with Miguel firing into the group, as well, to keep them pinned down in the rocks. At this point, the captain and his men come through the chokepoint into the river area, firing into the illegals, dropping two of them while they were trying to get to the American side of the river.

Most of the illegals made their way across the river onto the American side and were met by Jose, brandishing a gun to hold them there. The guys carrying the drugs threw the bundles into the river. The Border Patrol moved in from above and rounded up the illegals to load them up into a truck.

The captain ordered his men to set up a defensive position to contain the guerillas. His men went into the rocks to bring down the six that were left and hauled them away in one of the small trucks. The captain, seeing the illegals were on the other side of the river with the Border Patrol, went over to talk to the chief of the Border Patrol. "Thank you for helping us catch the people crossing into your country. We will take them from you now."

Jose, standing there listening to the captain, asked, "What are your intentions with these illegals, Captain?"

"To place them under arrest for trying to gain entry into America without the properly approved paperwork."

As the captain was saying this, Jose watched two soldiers grab the bundles from the river and load them into one of the other trucks.

"And what of the drugs, Captain?"

"We will keep them for evidence and turn them over to our government to dispose of as needed."

"I do not think that will be necessary, Captain. I believe I will let the Americans have the drugs for evidence. Order your men to release the drugs to the Americans right now," Jose said, smiling.

The captain knew that the drugs were on his side of the border, and he did not have to comply with Jose. He yelled at his men, "Raise your rifles on the Americans, and do not fire unless I tell you to."

The captain looked around, and even the guerillas had their weapons returned to them and pointed at the Border Patrol personnel from across the river. The captain, smiling, said, "I think we have the upper hand, senor."

At this point, the chief spoke up, "I think you don't understand your situation here very well, Captain," he continued, pointing up at the mountain. "We have sharpshooters watching you this very moment. All I need do is give them the signal and because you are on our side of the border, illegally, we have every right to shoot you where you stand."

"I think you lie to me, senor; I don't believe you have men ready to shoot," the captain said, smiling.

"Let me show you what I mean, Captain." The chief raised his hand and spoke into the radio, "Show and tell."

Two rounds hit in front of the captain between his legs; then came the reports from the rifles. The captain stepped back a little. "You are willing to kill me for the illegals and the drugs?"

"No, I don't think that is needed, but I will if you don't release the drugs right now."

Miguel and Lucas shouted out to the chief, "Any problems down there?"

This caught the captain off guard and he didn't know that there were Americans on the Mexican side, watching everything. He looked around, trying to see how many were in the rocks, but he couldn't tell.

The captain looked at the chief. "We have a problem with the Americans on our side of the border now."

"They have our government's permission to be in your country whereas you do not have that same permission, Captain," Jose said.

With that, Jose took his handgun out of its holster, walked up to the captain and put it next to the captain's temple, "Call your men off or I will personally blow your brains out right now, Captain," Jose insisted.

The captain stood there for a moment, smiled, and

ordered his men to stand down and give the drugs to the Americans. Lucas and Miguel carried the bundles to the other side of the river and set them down on the ground, where two Border Patrol men picked them up and took them away.

"Senor, you have created an international incident for our countries," said the captain.

"I don't think so, Captain. Oh, by the way, you're under arrest for murder, drug running, and being in the United States without permission," said Jose. Looking at the chief, Jose asked, "Would you mind holding the prisoner in one of your jails, seeing as how I don't have the men to take him back to Mexico right now?"

The chief nodded, "It would be my pleasure to do that for our neighboring country of Mexico. How long do you think he will be our guest?"

"Weeks, maybe months; it's hard to say at this time."

When he saw the captain being arrested by the Americans, the sergeant told his men to raise their weapons to fire. After firing his own gun at the Border Patrol chief and just as he was about to command his men to fire, the sergeant's head turned into a mist of red drops and brain matter and white bone as he dropped to the ground. His men, seeing what had happened to the sergeant, lowered their weapons and grabbed the body of the sergeant and put it in the bed of the truck. After that was done, the soldiers got back into their trucks and drove back to their base. By now, the captain was being loaded into one of the Border Patrol SUVs and was being accompanied by Jose. Jose looked at the body of the sergeant as it was being loaded into one of the trucks, "Captain, which one of your men fired the shot that killed the sergeant? You know, good soldiers are hard to find anymore."

Later that night, after getting back to Nogales, Lucas and Miguel sat in the office, writing the reports that needed to be turned in the next day. When evening came, Lucas was on his way out the door, getting ready to go to Amanda's soup kitchen for a bite to eat. Miguel was on his way home to Glendale to see Marissa and the kids. Smith was sitting in the office of the Border Patrol chief, drinking a cup of coffee and shooting the breeze about all that had happened earlier in the day. Each was waiting for the end of the day so they could go home, as well.

Jose was busy finishing up his report as the others were leaving so that he could go home, too. On his way out, Lucas stopped by to drop a candy bar off with Jose, "Good luck, and next time we get together you can buy the candy bars."

"Fair enough, my friend, until the next time," Jose said, smiling.

One more mission down, with one more piece of trash thrown in the garbage. One more day that everything ended on a high note for all involved. One more time the good guys won.

Chapter XIII

"Are you sure about this?" Evans asked the man.

The man nodded and said, "I'm very sure about it."

Linda and another agent listened to the confidential informant (CI) on the other side of the glass mirror explain how he found out that Johnny was the go-between for Frankie and the Organization that approved the hits on Buck, Rachael, and Miguel and their families.

He started by saying that he and Johnny were friends/cell mates when they were in prison together. After running into each other on the street, they decided to have a few drinks at the local bar. Johnny started running his mouth about knowing Frankie in prison. As the drinks started flowing, the CI listened to Johnny as he said, "We had to get permission from the Organization for the hit to be approved. When that was done, I headed out to the prison and told Frankie that it was a go. You know what, it was the only time I've ever seen Frankie smile since he was in prison."

Evans looked at him, "Would you be willing to testify to this in court?"

"I don't think so; I would be taken out by the Organization even before I got to court if I did testify," said the CI.

"I understand," said Evans, knowing that what the CI had said was correct.

Even if they could protect him, it would only be a matter of time before he was found dead.

"You're free to go and thank you for the information you gave us."

Linda tapped on the window as the other agent left the room escorting the CI back to the front door of the office to release him back out onto the streets. Evans sat there thinking about what the CI had said and whether the information was reliable. Linda walked into the room and sat down next to Evans. "What are you thinking about?"

"I was wondering if there was enough information from the CI to go after the Organization. All we have is information about the Organization that approved the hit, and it isn't enough to charge them and bring them to court, anyway. And seeing as how the hit never took place, it would be a waste of time and money for all involved."

"What is the name of this Organization, anyway?"

"It has no name but is based on the East Coast and runs all of the drug trade in Latin America and the United States, with ties to the Russian mafia, as well. I believe that would be like waking up a sleeping giant if we let Buck and Rachael go after the Organization."

"If we let them there may be a possibility that they

may be able to shake something loose that we can use to shut them down. Maybe we should turn it over to Buck and Rachael and let them do the legwork on it for us."

"We may just have to let them do it. I know that we don't want to know what happens to the Organization when they're done with it."

"I concur; I know it isn't going to be pretty and no one is going to get out alive in the Organization when Buck and Rachael are done with them," Linda said as she cringed in her seat.

"I'll text Buck to call me."

"I'm thinking that we're opening a can of whoop ass on the Organization and I'm wondering if they know what they've done?"

Chapter XIV

Buck and Rachael were on their way home to see their kids and relax from a week of working. Both of them were looking forward to a dip in their hot tub in the backyard, with the kids running around on the deck. When they got home, they changed from their uniforms into their bathing suits and ran to the hot tub to get in. Rachael was a little bit late getting in due to the cold drinks she had prepared for Buck and the kids.

Sitting on the edge of the tub letting her feet get used to the hot water, then sliding in the rest of the way, she sat there for a moment just enjoying the water and drinking her cold drink. Buck was already in the water completely, with his head back and eyes closed, just enjoying the moment, as well. All the cares of the world were gone and with the kids playing in the back yard, Buck said, "You know, it doesn't get any better than this."

"Mmm, I think you're right, and what a way to go."

They both sat in the tub for an hour, just relaxing in the water. It was Friday night and Rachael had picked up some DVD movies on the way home from work to watch with the kids later on in the evening. Dinner was pizza and Kool-Aid for everyone. As Buck sat down in his favorite chair, the youngest crawled onto his lap to watch the movie. Within an hour, Rachael was falling asleep and Buck was starting to doze, as well. Tugging on Rachael's big toe, he said it was time for the kids to go to bed. Taking them to their bedrooms was easy; they were fast asleep already and only needed to be covered up in their blankets.

Rachael and Buck looked at each one of their kids as they lay sleeping in their beds and smiled. Buck looked at Rachael, "You do good work. By the way, you know that they got all of my looks and brains, too."

"You wish they had your looks and brains," Rachael said, hitting Buck in the shoulder.

Buck pretended to be hurt by her remark. "Well, I NEVER."

"Keep it up, smarty, and you may never again," Rachael said, laughing.

It was quiet in the house and all was well for the night. They both headed to the bedroom and turned off the light. Friday was officially over for Buck and Rachael.

The next morning the kids came running into the master bedroom and jumped up and down on the bed, making it the official start of Saturday morning. Buck pulled the pillow over his head while Rachael put on her robe to take the kids to the kitchen for some cereal and milk. After getting the food down, she went back to bed and crawled in next to Buck, who was still sleeping. She nudged him, "Next Saturday you get out of bed to feed the kids."

By nine o'clock Buck and Rachael were awake and the Saturday chores began. For Buck, it was cleaning the TV room and stacking the dishes in the dishwasher. While Rachael got ready for the day, it was Buck's responsibility to watch the kids and get them dressed for the day's activities.

When Rachael was done, the kids were dressed and ready to go on their trip to see Miguel, Marissa, and their kids. Buck and Rachael had planned on going to see Foster and Elaine today at the hospital and then take the kids to spend time with Miguel and his family to see the Phoenix Zoo. Afterwards they were going to get together and have a picnic. A big day and a big outing had been planned for the two families to spend some time together.

Heading to the hospital first to check in on Foster and Elaine, they sat and visited for a little while to make sure Foster was doing fine. All Foster could think of was getting out of the hospital to go fishing. "I know I'd recover better if I were on my boat fishing."

Buck laughed, "There'll be plenty of time for that when they release you from the hospital."

"I don't know if I want them to release him from the hospital. It's the first time in years where the house is still clean after I went through and cleaned it. The kids are actually helping me keep it clean. If he comes back,

I'll never be able to keep it clean again," Elaine said with a smile.

"Are you trying to tell me I'm messier than the kids?" Foster asked.

"I didn't say it, but now that you mention it..."

"I think I'll move onto my boat and stay there," said Foster, acting hurt.

"That's what I forgot to tell you; I had the kids move all your stuff onto the boat since you have been in here. You can't believe how much room I have for my new sewing room I've created where your fishing gear used to be," said Elaine, digging at Foster.

"Well, we better be going now. I don't want to see a grown man cry," said Buck, laughing.

Rachael nodded and said to Elaine, "Good for you."

"Oh, sure, I get shot and my wife changes the house when I'm down and out and can't fight back. Where did you put my boat? I hope it's close to the house still," Foster said.

"Oh, I moved it down closer to the lake; in fact, it's right outside on the road leading into our subdivision. Ever since I put up a for rent sign on it, the phone just keeps ringing off the hook. The strangest thing, I went to go check on it yesterday, and it was gone! I hope whoever borrowed it returns it when they're done," Elaine said with a straight face.

"Oh, no, you didn't do that, did you?" Foster was now wondering.

"Well, I have to pay for the medical bills somehow. And I bought you a fancy golf cart to use, now that we have room on the driveway," Elaine said.

By now, Foster was ready to crawl out of bed and get dressed to go find his boat. Buck and Rachael were laughing at the two of them, watching Foster go through his gyrations over his boat.

"Wow, look at the time. We need to be going. You two have a good day and we'll be in touch for your divorce, if you need us," Rachael said.

"Buck, don't leave me here alone with this Jezebel," Foster said, laughing.

Elaine picked up a pillow off the bed next to him and threw it at him, laughing as she did. Rachael grabbed a pillow and threw it at Foster, as well, laughing at him.

"We're outta here," Buck said, smiling, while grabbing Rachael by the waist and pulling her away from the bed Foster was in.

"Let me at him, let me at him," Rachael said, laughing hysterically.

Foster started yelling for the nurse, "They're double-teaming me now."

The nurse came in and looked the situation over, asking Elaine, "Do you need any help fluffing up the pillows for your husband?"

The last words Foster said as Buck and Rachael were leaving were "You traitor, it's not time for a shot and you know it."

While walking out of the hospital, Buck got a message on his phone from Evans. As he read the text, Rachael looked at him, "What's up?"

"They found the Organization that approved the hit on us," Buck said as they walked to the truck. "I'll call him when we get back to the house," he said as he climbed into the cab.

The rest of the day was spent with the kids at the zoo, showing the animals to them. Miguel's kids were having the time of their lives, as well as Buck and Rachael's kids. By the end of the day everybody was tired and ready to go home and enjoy some hot dogs and hamburgers for dinner at Miguel's house. Loading the kids into the vehicles wasn't hard. All of them were tired and ready to sleep on the way back to Glendale. With the air conditioner on in the truck, Rachael started to doze, as well. Arriving home, the kids were getting their second burst of energy and were ready to eat. Miguel started up the grill and started cooking the hot dogs and hamburgers on the patio in the backyard. In about fifteen minutes the kids were eating, and Rachael and Marissa were slicing the watermelon for the kids to have when they were done with their hot dogs and hamburgers. Miguel and Buck sat outside in the shade, with the misters running to cool it down.

"Evans contacted me, to let me know that they had found the Organization that authorized putting the hit out on us today," Buck said.

"Who was it?" asked Miguel, anxious to know.

"I don't know as yet. I just received the text from Evans today while we were at the hospital. Don't tell Marissa yet; I don't want to upset her right now. As it stands, I will find out more when I can talk to Evans tomorrow."

Miguel nodded his head in agreement and sat there thinking about what he would like to do to get even with the Organization. "When do you think you will call him?"

"Most likely, I'll call tomorrow afternoon. I'll let you know what I find out as soon as I do."

"That's good, thanks for telling me," Miguel said, smiling with his eyes, not showing any feeling from his words.

By the end of the evening Buck and Rachael loaded their kids into the truck and after saying goodbye to Miguel, Marissa, and their grandkids, they drove back home.

The next day Buck called Evans, "What did you find out?"

"Well, it's like this, the Organization that approved the hit is based in New Jersey, and they run the drugs from Latin America into Europe and the U.S. with the help of the gangs and guerillas in each country they operate in."

"You say they're based in New Jersey?"

"Yes, they are working with the Russian mafia and

the Italian mafia, as well."

"So where's the office for this branch of the Organization?"

"They're spread out all over New York, Philadelphia, Cleveland, Los Angeles, Las Vegas and, of course, New Jersey. The one that you're interested in is located in New Jersey. The FBI has been interested in finding and disrupting their business for years; but with every attempt, witnesses disappear or we find them in the lakes and oceans with cement shoes on. And the ones that are left alive are afraid for their families to say anything."

As Buck sat listening, Rachael came in and sat down next to Buck to listen in. Buck switched the phone to speaker so that Rachael could hear what Evans had to say.

Evans continued speaking, "To be honest, you might be waking up a giant that could do more harm than good in taking it on. In other words, you might win the battle but lose the war."

Buck and Rachael listened to Evans as he spoke and, looking at each other, were wondering if it would be too much effort and time to go after the Organization, especially with it being based in New Jersey.

"Let us think about it and we'll let you know our plans when we decide what we're going to do," Buck said.

"Before I go, I'll let you know that this will be like

what you guys did for us in Colombia. I think we could support you in this endeavor with some manpower and whatever else you needed to go after this Organization. That being said, you would have to become FBI agents to get our support from the field offices out there on the East Coast."

"All right, like I said, we'll let you know what we decide. Good night."

"Good night."

Buck and Rachael sat there for a moment without saying anything. The night was coming on and the coolness of the evening was starting to be felt. Buck took Rachael by the hand and looked into her eyes, "What do you want to do about what Evans said?"

Sitting there for a moment, mulling it over in her mind, she said, "I'm not sure what to do about it. If we stand down, somebody else may come along and try to take us out, and maybe next time we won't be as lucky as we were this last time."

"I know what you mean. Frankie will keep trying until he is successful. We can't hide from them and pretend it's not going to happen and continually be stressed out worrying about Miguel and the kids getting hurt."

"I think we have no choice in the matter. The way I see it, if we don't try to stop them, we will end up being dead, anyway."

"I agree with you. If we die, I'd rather go down

fighting than hiding, wondering when it's going to happen."

"What about Miguel, what do we tell him?"

"The truth. We tell him what Evans said to us and let him decide what he wants to do for himself."

"I agree with you on this."

Buck called Miguel to let him know what they had learned from Evans' phone call. He withheld his decision, not wanting to influence Miguel in any way. Miguel listened to Buck and didn't say a word until he was finished, and then only after, Buck asked, "What are your thoughts on this?"

"When do we leave for New Jersey? I can't be gone all the time, wondering if Marissa is alive every day while I'm out there in the desert fighting against the same kind of people trying to kill me and my family."

"I agree with you, Miguel. Your mother and I have decided to stand and fight these people. I didn't tell you our decision until you knew all of the facts and had some time to think about it yourself."

"There's nothing to think about; we either fight them on our terms or we sit and wait for them to come here, never knowing when or where they'll show up on our doorstep. So when do we go to New Jersey?"

"I'll let you know sometime this week after I tell Evans about our decision to go."

The next day being Tuesday, Buck called Evans first thing when he got to his office. When Evans picked up the phone, realizing who it was, he asked, "What have you decided to do?"

"We decided to go to New Jersey and sort this out with the Organization."

"I thought that would be your answer, and I already have the paperwork filled out for you and Rachael to become FBI agents. You should be ready to go in about three days from now."

"We talked to Miguel about what you told us last night, and he wants to go with us, as well. Is that a problem for you guys?"

"Let me look into it. I personally don't see a problem with it, but it isn't my decision as far as he goes. I should know in about a day or so. I'll let you know when I hear something."

"Fair enough for me."

Buck called Rachael on her phone and asked her to come in to his office. She arrived five minutes later. "What's up?"

"We're a go for the trip to New Jersey, and we're waiting on the FBI higher-ups on allowing Miguel to go."

"That's good to know. When do we start this adventure?"

"Three days, near as I can tell. Looks like another vacation to the East Coast on the government," Buck said, smiling.

"Oh boy, another fun filled trip to the big city. I can

hardly wait."

Buck and Rachael had a lot to do to prepare for the trip and also let the undersheriff know what was going on. He would run the county business while Buck was gone on "vacation" once again. At the end of three days, Evans contacted Buck. "Your badges will be in the New Jersey office when you get there, and for Miguel, as well. It took some doing, but they thought it might be best to have him come along and keep an eye on you two."

Buck laughed, "Thank you for pulling it off for us."

"Don't thank me it was the work you guys did in Colombia and Honduras that got you approved for the trip to Jersey City. Just don't get killed or hurt out there; I want your godchildren to know who their godparents are."

"I'll try not to get killed out there, not only for you but for me, as well."

"Good deal. I'll see you guys when you get to New Jersey. Your tickets should arrive in today's mail. See you there."

Buck called Miguel, "You've been approved to go so you'll need to be ready to go, hopefully by tomorrow."

"Not a problem; I'll be ready," Miguel said.

The hard part for Miguel would be telling Marissa about going to New Jersey and leaving her alone again with the kids. He waited until the kids were down for a nap. Then he told her about the trip to New Jersey, and that he would be going with Buck and Rachael to go after the Organization that tried to kill her and the kids.

She thought about it for a little bit. "Get them all for me, will you. They tried to kill me and my kids; get them all."

Surprised by Marissa's comment, Miguel put his arms around her and held her, promising, "I will do my best to get them all."

Chapter XV

At eight-thirty in the morning Buck and Rachael were at Miguel's house, loading Miguel's suitcase into the back of the truck as Miguel was saying goodbye to Marissa and the kids. Buck and Rachael said their goodbyes, as well, to their grandkids and Marissa, once everything was loaded into the truck. Their flight to New Jersey was to leave at one o'clock in the afternoon, but they had to be there two hours early; and not knowing anything of the security checks at the airport, they decided to leave early to be sure there would be no snafus in the process.

Once through security and waiting at their gate, they sat there watching the TV monitor to kill some time before boarding their flight. All at once, Miguel stood up and walked over to a man walking in their direction. He put his arms around the guy and walked back with him to where Buck and Rachael were sitting. Miguel was surprised to see Lucas there at the airport, "What are you doing here?"

"Smith thought that I needed to go with you guys to make sure you didn't get into any trouble without me. Seeing as how we are a team and this is an FBI operation, Smith let me go, too. I want you to know that

Amanda was not happy with me leaving her again to go to the East Coast."

"Tell her I'll make it up to her when we get back. Mom, Dad, this is Lucas, my cohort in crime," Miguel said.

Buck and Rachael stood up, shaking his hand, Buck exclaimed, "Welcome to the party."

In an hour, the ticket agent started calling out seat assignments to the general public. Once on board the plane, they flew to Denver and caught another flight to Philadelphia, then on to New Jersey. The total time on the plane was about six hours, and after landing in New Jersey, they were met by a man showing a card with their names on it. The man introduced himself, "Welcome to New Jersey. My name is James Alexander, but most people call me Jim."

After loading all their gear into the van, Jim drove them to a hotel close to the Trump Tower, near the boardwalk.

"I will pick you guys up at eight am sharp tomorrow morning; in the meantime, enjoy your stay and I'll see you later," Jim said.

As they got settled into their rooms, Buck and Rachael in one room and Miguel and Lucas in another room, they unpacked some of their stuff to see them through till the next day. Once they were settled, Miguel and Lucas met Buck and Rachael in the foyer of the hotel.

"I'm starved. Do you guys want to try the Trump

Plaza and see if they have a buffet?" Lucas said.

"Works for me and the girl I go with," replied Buck as Rachael nodded in agreement.

As they walked over towards the Plaza, they noticed all the restaurants located next to the hotel. They decided to eat at one of the local eateries there, instead. From where they sat, they could see the lights of Brooklyn, New York, or lower Manhattan. The view was breathtaking for a couple of country tourists taking in the city for the first time. Buck was looking through one of the realtor magazines and was surprised at the cost of living in the Trump Plaza and the surrounding buildings. The prices started at a little over a half a million all the way up to over a million dollars for a condo of maybe a 100-square-foot room.

Buck was shocked by the prices and how close everything was here in the city. He started to feel claustrophobic, even on the streets, as they walked home from dinner. Lucas and Miguel were totally blown away by the size of the skyscrapers and how tall they were. Miguel had never seen anything like this before, even in Colombia. Buck and Rachael smiled at the way the two of them took it all in.

The next morning at eight o'clock, Jim Alexander picked them up and took them to the FBI headquarters in New Jersey. Upon getting out of the van, Evans and Linda were there to meet them all. Shaking hands with hugs all around, the group went through the security doors and into the main offices of the building. Evans and Linda introduced them to the lead Special Agent in Charge, Bob Kennedy, who said, "I've heard so much about you two and the good work you did in Arizona and South America and, of course, Las Vegas."

Buck and Rachael blushed and smiled at his remarks.

Then, he turned his gaze to Miguel and Lucas, "Did you guys really pour sugar into the trucks' fuel tanks in Mexico?"

Lucas and Miguel looked at each other and stood there, smiling. "Yes."

"Ingenious thinking. All your reputations precede you guys as being able to think on your feet and not waiting for input when the timeline is short. Very impressive, indeed, and you're the kind of people we need on this case we're about to start. Now, if you will follow me, please, into the next room," Kennedy said.

As they walked into the room, there was a big conference table with people sitting around it. Kennedy had Buck and Rachael sit in the chairs behind the table, with Lucas and Miguel sitting behind them, against the wall.

Kennedy introduced Buck and Rachael. "These two people destroyed the Organization's hold on Las Vegas, found two leaks in our Miami office, and destroyed about a million or so dollars in drugs before hitting the streets in America. The other two sitting behind them were instrumental breaking up a human and drug trafficking problem in Mexico last week. Now, they have all volunteered to be members on the team, after they were involved with an attempted assassination of Miguel and his family. Their mission here is to find who the person is that approved the hit on them from the Organization and take them down."

Kennedy let his words sink into his audience before he started speaking again. With everybody looking at him now, he continued, "We think with their abilities to think outside the box, they may give us a fresh, or at least, a different perspective on the Organization and assist us in bringing them down. They will be assigned as FBI agents to the team and work as a unit, going in and finding the weak links in the Organization and exploiting them to our advantage."

After Kennedy's speech, he had each person sitting at the table introduce themselves to Buck and Rachael, explaining their part in the operation. The first to speak was Peter Knight. "I work with the DEA and have the street connections to where the drug dealers are."

Next was Joe Cagney. "I'm a CIA analyst whose job is to keep a pulse on the different drug places in Europe and Latin America and watch the drug flow from these countries into our country."

The next person was Claudia Smith. "I'm a forensics computer specialist from the NSA. I'll be involved with the money-laundering aspect of the drug empire. I'll be feeding you guys information while you're out in the field, i.e., the places we think the drug money is being laundered and where to stop it."

And last, but not least, was Race Benttin, the lead agent from the FBI for the joint-operation team. "I'll be directing the entire operation out in the field, as well as here in the office. At this point, we have made some inroads into the Organization; we just need to capitalize on them to bring it down."

"One person I would like to introduce to you is Mike Childs. He's with the U.S. Marshal's Office and he'll be working with us on the street, assisting us with known gang members selling drugs," Race said.

Mike stood up and smiled and then quickly sat down again.

Kennedy took over. "From now on, you will be working from this office and all decisions will be made from here before anything goes down. Buck and the others will be staying on McGuire Air Force Base for lodging purposes only; leastwise, your stuff will be located there."

Evans and Linda, walked up to Buck and Rachael after the briefing. "We really want to say how much we appreciate what you're doing for us here. I must tell you that, before you find out for yourselves, Race is kinda like a micro manager from hell; be prepared to not have the freedom you normally would have when you were on your own working together."

"Thanks for the heads up," said Rachael.

"We'll take you back to the hotel so that you can pick up your gear and get it to McGuire Lodging for you," Linda said.

Race Benttin came over to Buck and Rachael. "I hear you like to play loose when you're out in the field. I'll let you know, right now, I won't tolerate any of that from any of you here on in. It will be by the book all the way, do you understand?"

"We understand, and do you want us to call you "sir," or will that be necessary?" asked Buck.

Race just stood there a moment and, after a second, walked away. Linda and Evans smiled, as did Lucas and Miguel. Rachael looked at Buck, nudging him. "Tell me, where did you get the training on the 'How to Win Friends and Influence People' course?"

"I couldn't help myself; did I say something wrong?" Buck asked, jokingly.

With Evans driving, they took the van back to the hotel and picked up their suitcases and other gear and then headed out to McGuire Air Force Base for their lodging. After everybody got settled in their rooms, Evans took them back to the FBI office and handed them the keys for the two cars he had waiting for them. Miguel and Lucas would have one car; the other car would go to Buck and Rachael. As they walked back into the office, Linda brought a sack out and handed each of them an FBI shield for them to carry. "The real briefing will happen tomorrow morning; in the meantime, here is some information for you to read tonight."

The next morning at eight o'clock, the briefing began with the drug business on the entire East Coast of the U.S. and the part the Organization played in it. This part of the briefing was conducted by CIA analyst Joe Cagney, using maps and PowerPoint slides indicating the types of drugs and gangs used to distribute the drugs.

"The Organization is considered to be the key player involved with Transnational Drug Trafficking, which operates from Latin America and feeds drugs to Europe and the U.S. The Organization works with the Latin American countries like Brazil, Honduras, Mexico, Nicaragua, and others. It's the brains behind the drug distribution network, using street gangs to peddle drugs throughout the U.S.," stated Joe.

After a fifteen-minute break, Joe picked up from where he left off. "The drugs are protected by EIN (gang drug security) or PACM (drug distribution) located in Colombia. According to reports, the EIN would provide security for drug development and PACM would control the departure ports. The drugs would leave either on fast boats or through commercial shipping that took the drugs to countries in the Caribbean islands and parts of Central America for further distribution to Europe and the United States. The gangs involved in this are based in Central America and are here in the United States illegally, working the street corners selling the drugs to anybody and everybody."

Race took over the briefing on the gangs with new Intel they found. "These gangs are considered to be very well organized. The leadership of the gangs, even though in prison, are still controlling what's going on in the East and West Coasts of the United States. They actually had a meeting once in New York, as a coalition, to discuss and decide their next move regarding expanding their influence in other mid-western and southern states. Their main business is the selling of drugs, but they have been linked to murder, rape, and theft. All indications show that they are starting to be bolder because of the money to be made in all aspects of the drug trade and their willingness to do what is necessary to get their piece of the pie."

Buck raised his hand. "So what is your plan for going after the Organization? Are we going from the bottom up or from the top down?"

Claudia Smith stood up, "I would like to answer that question, if I may. We want to hurt them where it counts; that is, their money source. If we can find that, we can freeze their assets and shut them down completely. By so doing, the impact will be felt all over their circle of influence."

"In other words, we steal their computer and disrupt their Organization," Race said.

"Do we know where they keep their computer and such?" asked Miguel.

"The computers are kept in what we would call their headquarters in New Jersey, which is under guard 24/7 with only permission given by the guy in charge to access the computer. His name is Danny 'The Jackal' Thompson. He is the key player in the Organization and is for the most part untouchable, with his guards always hanging around him as security. Even at night, there are at least two guards watching over him. Are there any questions?" Race asked.

"I want to know who is going after the computer," said Rachael.

"At this point, we don't have anybody who can break in and take it without being compromised and blowing our operation."

"What is it that you want us to do while we're here?" asked Lucas.

"I want you guys to go after the computer and Danny the Jackal and bring him in for questioning," Race said.

"How do you expect us to do that?" Buck asked.

"By the book, of course," Race said sarcastically. Then he continued, "You will follow the protocols in going after Danny and anybody else that gets in your way. If you need a warrant, we will get a warrant based on something substantial."

By now, Buck and Rachael knew that this Race was going to be a pain in the ass for the team.

"Just how many of these kinds of operations have you been on as the team lead?" Rachael asked.

The question caught Race off guard and, at first, he didn't know how to answer. After a minute he volunteered, "This is my first one as team lead. I have been on at least three other operations as part of the team."

This time, Buck asked the question, "How many of them were successful?"

"What difference does that make?" Race snapped back.

"If I have to depend on you to back me up, I just want to make sure you <u>will</u> back me up or anybody else on the team. We're talking our lives here, not just your protocol."

Race didn't know how to respond to this, and there was a moment of silence in the room.

Buck continued, "If I can't depend on you to make the right decisions in the field, we're going home tomorrow. We'll get Danny the Jackal our own way."

With that, Buck stood up, as did the rest of the team, and started walking out the door of the conference room. Race didn't know what to do; he stood there as he watched his team filing out of the room. The other members of the team sat there in total silence, watching Race to see what he was going to do. Finally, Race realized that this game of who blinks first was won by Buck and his team. At this point, Race yelled, "Wait a minute."

Buck looked at him, "You have something to say?"

"Would you please come back into the room and sit down for a moment."

Race knew everything was on the line for this operation, and he had to handle this situation like he would like it to be handled. He also knew that without Buck and his team the mission was over before it started, and so would be his career.

"Yes, I do have something to say. I want you and your people to understand I'm in charge of this team and you are not. Do you understand what I'm saying to you?"

Buck, who had already sat down, stood up again and started walking to the door. Before going through it, he looked at Race. "Whether you realize it or not, we are the team and you are nothing to us. That being said, if you want to work together on this, you will shut up and listen to me and or Rachael; that is, if you want to live through this operation. Do you understand what I'm telling you?"

Race didn't know what to say; still standing there, Buck asked again, "Do you understand what I'm telling you? It's your call, Race; none of us are going to die for you."

This time, Claudia and Mike and Joe got up and walked over to where Buck and the rest of the team were standing and stood with them.

By now, Race was beside himself and didn't know

how to handle the situation. No one had ever pushed this hard against him before, and nobody had ever stood up to him like this before. He knew if this operation worked or failed, it would be decided right here and right now. His only choices were, one, swallow his pride and consent to working as a team or, two, walk away and never be put in charge of anything again and watch his career die on the vine. Thinking on these two options, he finally realized he would be the one who would need to change his attitude and have to prove himself to the team.

"I'm wrong, and you're right. Instead of trying to be a bull in a china shop, I need to listen and learn from people who have been out there in the real world. Will you work with me on this operation?" Race asked, humbled by what had just happened.

"Welcome aboard, then," Buck said.

With everybody seated again, the meeting took on a totally different tone, and everybody actually started working together to figure out which way to attack the problems of getting into the Organization.

"I think I know someone who can assist us in getting through the security at the Organization's place of business," the marshal said.

With that, Buck said, "Take Lucas and Miguel with you, just in case you run into any problems."

"Claudia, do you have any friends that you can trust to hack into the computers and start bleeding the

Organization's money from their bank account and send it to the gang leaders who sell the drugs?"

"Yes, I do, and I'll get on it right away."

"Good, take Joe with you. I'm thinking if we can siphon the money and put it into one of the gang's accounts, that might start a war with their peddlers on the street. Joe, I need you to follow the trail of drugs and find a way, with Claudia's help, to freeze their assets and let the money be found in the Organization's bank account in one of Treasure Island's banks. Make sure the trail is easy to follow for the suppliers."

Joe nodded his head and went with Claudia to figure out how to break into the Organization's accounts.

Buck looked at Rachael and Race. "Our job is to get the computer in the Organization's building, either by stealing it or downloading all of the memory on the hard drive and use it against the Organization. We need to be able to figure a way to break in without them knowing we were there; any ideas on how to do that?"

"If Claudia and Joe have any luck, they may be able to do it for us," Rachael said.

"That way we may not have to break in," Race added.

Buck thought about this for a minute. "You may be right; however, we need to be ready with a plan, just in case, anyway."

Buck looked at Race, "Do you have the floor plans for their building with you?"

Race thought for a moment, "I know where we can

get some up-to-date plans really quick." And with that, he took off to go get them.

Buck hollered out, "As soon as you can, bring them here and we'll start going over them."

By midday, Race was back with the plans. "I brought the original plans, as well as the newer plans. I was thinking maybe there might be a change in the before-and-after to look at for an opening somewhere."

"Good thinking, Race. We may find a security blind spot somewhere in the building that we can capitalize on."

"Do you have any actionable warrants on the Organization we can use right now?" Rachael asked.

"I think most of what we got is more hearsay than fact. We need to dig up some more stuff on the Organization to be able to act on the warrants," Race said.

"Maybe Miguel and Lucas and the marshal can find some credible dirt to use in getting the warrants for us," Buck said.

With the delegation of tasks completed, Buck turned to Race. "When do you want to meet again?"

"How about in a couple of days, to see if there is any progress being made in the computer arena? That being said, be ready to meet at any time if something new comes up."

"It's your call, but it sounds good to me."

At this point, Lucas and Miguel left with the U.S.

Marshal to see what they could find out on the street. Claudia and Joe were gone already, so it was on Buck, Rachael, and Race, to find a weakness in the floor plans for the Organization's building. After spending an hour looking over the new and old floor plans, they found an interesting difference between the two plans. On the old plans, they found a skylight opening that was over the main part of the office. In the new plans, the skylight was removed, supposedly closed up. Buck and Rachael thought this might be the building's weak spot. If they covered it up but maybe didn't fill it in, they could access it through the roof.

Buck looked at Race, "We need to go and see for ourselves, and then we can proceed from there."

Rachael nodded in agreement, "The real question is, how are we going to do that without being caught?"

"How about we create a diversion on the main street in front of the building and draw their attention to that, and then we can send somebody up the fire escape ladder in the back," Race suggested.

"I like it, but what can we do to create it?" asked Buck.

"How about an auto accident or maybe a chemical spill in sewage lines in which everybody has to be evacuated from the building for safety concerns? Once they're out of the building, we go in as a hazmat team to check it out," said Rachael.

Both Race and Buck liked the thought of the chemical

spill as a diversion.

"With someone on the roof, we can lower that person in to do what needs to be done with the computer. They can copy the hard drive and then be brought back up to the roof with the copy of the hard drive. They just need to complete the task as if nobody had been there," Buck added.

"How do we get the hazmat and the police to play along with our diversion? I'm afraid that if we tell them what we're doing, the word might get back to the Organization," Rachael said.

"So let's make it real for all involved," Race replied.

"What do we use in order to get hazmat here without getting caught for faking an incident?" Buck asked.

"Simple, let's treat it as a possible terrorist act and we show up as part of the hazmat team to investigate the situation," Race offered.

"It all sounds good to me. What do we use to create a panic for real in order to clear a building?" Buck asked, being pleased with his team for coming up with the ideas.

"How about we use a stink bomb and run it through their heating and ventilation system. We can let it loose from the top of the roof," Rachael replied.

They all laughed at the idea, picturing in their minds what would happen with the smell. Everybody would come pouring out of the building, coughing and gagging from the smell. The team then would walk in with hazmat gear on to clear the building and find a toilet-paper roll with the smell emanating from it. The building would take an hour to vent out with the windows open. By then, the team would be done and gone and the leaders of the Organization couldn't go back in for another hour, none the wiser and no questions asked, except for who planted the stink bomb.

"What do we need to create a stink bomb?" asked Race.

"All we need is ammonium sulfide," said Buck, smiling. "We could make it by mixing some home-grown ingredients like sulphur and lime in a big pot, add water, heat it up. Of course, this will need to be made outside so we don't kill ourselves with the smell. The best part is, the liquid is vile but it is not poison. We could use a cloth or a roll of toilet paper and put it inside the vent and wait."

"So, how do you know about all of this?" asked Rachael.

"What did you think I learned while I was in college?" replied Buck.

"That explains a lot."

Once the plan was set up, it now became a thing of implementing it. With that in mind, Buck, Rachael, and Race went to the address of the Organization's headquarters and looked around the area for another building close by. Getting to the top of the building they chose was easy, just had to climb the 20 flights of stairs to the roof. Getting out on the roof and looking across to the top of the Organization's roof was simple enough. Using binoculars, they scanned the roof top quickly. They saw an air conditioning unit, with the door from the stairwell nearby. No guards were on top of the roof, but there were security cameras located on each corner of the building, all pointing in towards the roof of the building.

Buck looked at the security cameras and started cussing. He hadn't thought about security cameras up on the roof and wasn't sure how to take them out without letting the guards in the building know that their team was there.

Race, picked up his binoculars and to see what Buck was concerned about, "We still go and do what we have planned; we just clear the building first before we go in to get the computer hard drive. That way, nobody is watching the cameras from inside."

"So how do we get them out of the building?" Rachael asked.

"By using two stink bombs instead of one. We plant one inside the building from up on top; the other one we plant below the building inside the sewage pipe or the electrical panel. The effect will be the same, but the bottom bomb will clear out the people inside first," Race replied.

"What happens if the security people decide to stay in the building after the stink bomb is planted?" Buck asked.

"The hazmat team will go in and clear every room inside the building before our team will descend from the top to copy the hard drive," replied Race.

"We just need to make sure that the same people going in are the same ones coming out, just in case somebody's paying attention," Rachael said.

Leaving the adjoining building and going back to their office, they located the city plans of the street layout below the Organization's building. After commandeering the blueprints, they studied the layout and found a direct line to the building for sewage with a control valve in line with the piping. To plant the stink bomb would require setting up a city truck with maintenance people working around the manhole. Then drilling a hole into the sewage pipe big enough to allow the fumes to travel up into the building wouldn't be hard; it would be just a matter of time and the right size of spout needed to feed the stink-bomb fumes inside the pipe.

Now, it was a matter of getting everything set up for stealing the hard drives. They would borrow the hazmat suits from the Department of Homeland Security. The city maintenance truck would be easy to get, seeing as how the FBI had used them before on other stakeouts. The question was, who would be the one going down from the top of the building into the office to retrieve the hard drive's information?

Buck first thought of Lucas or Miguel, as they were younger than the rest of them and therefore more agile than any of the old-timers. They could slip in and out without too much worry. Getting on and off the roof was the next long pole in the tent. Using a zipline from one building would work going in, but getting off of the building would be the hard part.

"How about we cut the zipline going to the building and use it to climb back up to the roof from where we started?" Rachael suggested.

"They could use the same stairs going up as they did to go copy the hard drive," said Buck.

"Oh yeah, I didn't think of that. Do you think we could have them be part of the hazmat team that went in? That way, they could come out through the building as part of the team. That way, they come out the same way we went in," said Rachael.

"Good idea, nobody is going to keep track of the hazmat crew going in and out, as long as we are not grouped together," Race said.

"We better get some of Mike's friends in on this, as well," said Buck.

With that in mind, the plan was put into motion. Lucas, Miguel, and Mike came back after being called by Buck. They showed up at the office, waiting with Race and Rachael while Buck talked to Claudia and Joe.

After gathering the team together in the meeting room, Buck let Race explain to the team what they wanted to do regarding downloading the hard drive.

"We'll start at two o'clock am with Lucas and Miguel using a zipline from the adjacent building to the top of the Organization's building. They will each be carrying a hazmat suit for themselves. The first thing Lucas and Miguel will need to do is disable the security cameras. We figure if you two stay close to one side of the roof and make your way to the door and let yourselves in, only one camera will need to be taken care of."

Miguel looked at Lucas. "I have an idea for the camera that should work."

"Mike will be with Claudia on the roof of the adjacent building to pull the zip line back up to where they are. Once that's complete, Mike and Claudia will need to come back down so that Mike will be ready to be part of the city maintenance crew. At this point, we'll need to have a city maintenance truck ready to go first thing in the morning. Joe, Mike, and I will be part of the maintenance team. We'll launch the stink bombs at the same time, exactly at seven o'clock am. Make sure to give yourselves 15 minutes before you start down into the building. I'll cut the power to the building to ensure the alarms will not work. Mike, you will be the lead on the maintenance team, as far as handling any complaints. Buck, you and Rachael will be the hazmat team with your gear on, ready to go as soon as the people clear the building." Buck and Rachael nodded in agreement. "You'll need a hazmat truck for you to drive up to the site." said Race.

"Not a problem; we will use the command post truck from the FBI," Buck said.

"Lucas and Miguel will look for the computer and, once finding it, they'll do the download of the hard drive." Looking at Miguel and Lucas, Race said, "Make sure you bring enough thumb drives to capture all of the material on the hard drive."

Lucas and Miguel agreed with Race, "We'll bring at least five thumb drives with us," Miguel said.

Claudia, you will be one of the spectators watching what's going on. When Miguel and Lucas are finished, they will come out of the building, head to the FBI command post truck, and discard their hazmat suits. Make sure you stagger coming out of the building. I'll need you to bring them back here in your car to lock up the drives. You will then bring Lucas and Miguel back to the site and have Lucas and Miguel be part of the security team, just in case something goes wrong."

Claudia nodded, "This is pretty exciting for a computer geek."

"The stink bombs will eventually dissipate over a couple of hours, giving you guys a chance to close up shop and head out. Mike will be the face-man for whoever is in charge of the building security. Your job is to make sure no one goes in or comes out without a hazmat suit on."

Lucas looked at Race, "I think this will work, but I

have to say I've never been on a zipline before."

"Not to worry, you'll do fine; it's the abrupt stop at the bottom that gets everybody at least once," Joe said, smiling.

Lucas thought about that for a moment before feigning laughter at Joe.

"Are there any questions about what we're doing?" Race asked. After seeing no hands in the air he continued, saying, "If all goes well, we should be done by nine am."

"One final thought before any of you leave: If you find somebody inside the building, escort them out before you do anything," Race said.

Buck added, "This is a go for tonight so be ready for your parts and work it out in your minds so that there will be no surprises for you. Show time is one o'clock am."

The rest of the day was spent getting the equipment ready for the mission and lining up the trucks and the rest of the equipment needed for each of their parts. Mike called a few of his buddies and coordinated with them as spectators to enforce security around the back and sides of the building. The city police would be there for crowd control for only in front of the building.

Having a checklist, Race and Buck went through it to make sure everything they would need would be available. Making sure everything was in order, they took a break and Race found a place to sleep till it was time to go. Miguel went to the park looking for a statue and camped there for an hour, enjoying the weather and how nice it was. Lucas was on the phone talking to Amanda, and they were lost in their own world. After leaving Race, Buck found Rachael talking to Claudia, trying to keep her calm and focused on the night's activities. Joe was busy with a game on his laptop.

By one o'clock am, the team was assembled and ready for their parts in the mission. Miguel and Lucas were dressed in black clothes with harnesses on and Mike and Claudia were dressed in regular clothes, carrying a rope with a treble hook on one end. The angle of the adjacent building where they would launch the zipline from was higher than the Organization's roof, and a good throw of the treble hook would catch the lip of the Organization's roof, thus securing the zipline between the two buildings.

The trucks were all ready and sitting in the garage inside the secured federal parking lot, with the hazmat suits ready for Buck and Rachael to wear. The hard hats and orange vests for Mike and Race were located inside the city maintenance vehicle.

The stink bombs had been created by Buck and Miguel and were sealed in two separate containers. One container was for Lucas and Miguel and the other for Race and Mike to carry with them.

Chapter XVI

At precisely two am, Miguel and Lucas were watching Mike shoot the rope with a grappling hook gun onto the other building. Once the rope was secure, Miguel and Lucas swung their legs over the edge of the building, and using their pulleys and harnesses, they released the brakes on the pullies and started sliding down the rope to the Organization's rooftop. Miguel had gone first and told Lucas to wait a minute before coming over. Miguel, once landing on the other building, took out a brown sack and, taking some stuff out of it, covered the one camera with it, blocking the lens from seeing anything. After this was done, he signaled for Lucas to come over, when he had landed on the other building, Lucas asked, "What were you doing?"

"I was taking care of the camera for us by putting bird crap all over the camera lens."

Lucas stood there a moment shaking his head. "At least, that explains why you went to the park earlier today. The things we do for our country."

Picking the lock to the door that led to the stairwell was easy. Once on the inside, they waited for the time to change into their hazmat suits. Lucas cradled the backpack between his legs on the floor so that the stink bomb wouldn't accidentally break open too soon.

Mike and Claudia pulled the rope up and took themselves back down to the street garage and sat in the car, waiting for the next step. This would give them time to catch their breath from all the flights of stairs they had to climb up and down.

At six am, Mike said to Claudia, "Act two starting, exit stage left."

Claudia smiled at Mike's comment, "Good luck and good hunting."

Mike went to the federal building's secure parking lot and picked up a city maintenance truck with Joe and Race waiting for him. Arriving at the front of the building and setting up a work zone around the truck, they raised the manhole cover and went down inside to find the connection for the sewer line. After fifteen minutes, they were set to drill and pour the stink bomb through the drilled hole into the sewage pipe, then place a piece of cork in the drilled hole so the fumes wouldn't stink them out.

Buck and Rachael were in the command post van, waiting for the call from Mike or Race to come. Already dressed in their hazmat suits, leastwise to their waists, they sat there drinking their coffee. Neither of them were talking, except for what needed to be said for the mission. The adrenaline rush was already starting for all the players involved. Mike was alert, as he kept checking his watch every five minutes. Joe was looking at his computer as he wired the electrical system to it, getting ready to shut off the power to the security system inside the Organization's building.

At seven am, both Miguel and Race released the stink bombs. It only took a minute for the smell to permeate the whole building, going up the sewer system and down through the elevator shaft. Race called for the hazmat team to be ready. As the smell got stronger, the people inside the building started coming out the front doors.

Being so early in the morning, only the night security team was on duty. The security chief came over and asked Mike, "What happened?"

"We hit a gas pocket down in one of the pipes and it blew back up into the building. We've already called Hazmat and they should be on their way to check it out for us."

Buck and Rachael got there in five minutes and had already taken control of the situation by having their sensors working, looking for the leak. Buck, after checking the manhole area, said, "It's got to be in the building; we're going in."

"I'll go with you," said the security chief.

"No, you're not, Chief, we don't know what's in there and I'm not taking a civilian with me. That's why there are two of us going in. You stay out here. We'll be back as soon as we can."

The security chief was not pleased about not being

able to go in with the Hazmat team but understood why he had to wait outside.

Buck and Rachael went in through the front doors fully dressed in their hazmat suits, reading their sensors as they went. Lucas and Miguel were dressed in their hazmat suits, looking for the main computer hub. The smell was so bad in the building it was permeating their suits and causing their eyes to water. As both teams went through each room looking for the computer system, they met on the third floor in front of a door marked "Private." Buck opened it, "Bingo, we found the computer room."

It was only a few minutes, and all of the hard drives had been copied onto three of the thumb drives. Buck, talking to Race through their earwigs, confirmed that the download was complete. Now, getting out of the building for each hazmat team without being counted was the next step.

"Mike, you need to entertain the security chief and his men to divert their attention from the front door," said Race.

Finding the security chief and his men, Mike had them come over and get checked for anything contagious from the gases while they had been inside the building.

The bathrooms were the worst place for the gas. It would bubble up through the water in the toilets like a hot tub with the pumps on and the gas would spread from there. Race, watching the security people getting checked, gave the signal for Lucas and Miguel to come out. As they stepped out of the building, they hurried into the hazmat truck and stripped off their suits. They took them off and put them into plastic bags, then carried them over to where Claudia had been waiting. She then led the way to her car and popped open the trunk, dumping their plastic bags in. All three of them got into her car and left the scene.

Arriving back at the Federal Building, they dropped off the thumb drives into the IT section for a download to the FBI computers. They got back into the car and returned to the site and pretended to be curious passersby watching the show. By now, the security chief and his men had been checked and found to be within tolerable limits for humans.

Five minutes later, Race gave the all clear signal, "When you're ready, come on out."

Buck acknowledged Race's message and both Buck and Rachael came through the doors, and as they started to take off their hazmat suits, they gave the all-clear signal for everybody to pack it up and head back to the office.

The security chief came over and asked Buck, "When can we go back in?"

"When the smell goes away; it's pretty strong in there right now. I would give it an hour before going in and I would suggest you open all the windows to air it out when you do go in."

By now, Joe had the security system back up and running normally, and the hole on the sewer pipe was plugged with a cork and duct tape. Mike, acting as the chief for the city, said to his men, "I think we're done here. It will take some time for the air to clear inside the building, but it should be safe to go in once the fumes have dissipated."

Joe and Race started taking down all the safety equipment and closed the manhole. They left the scene in the city maintenance truck, following Buck and Rachael, who were driving the hazmat truck back to the office.

The security chief ordered his men to get some gas masks that they could wear inside the building till the air was clear. As it was, it would take approximately two hours before anybody else could go in without a mask. Once getting their masks, the security team went in and checked all the floors and, opening the windows, found nothing out of place. When Danny "The Jackal" came in, he was briefed on what had happened and told everything was secure in the building.

By nine am, everybody was back at the federal building down in the IT room, waiting to see what they had downloaded from the computer thumb drives. As everybody stood around, they were most interested in making sure that the information on the hard drives was able to be downloaded onto the FBI's computer to be evaluated. Everybody knew it would take weeks to decipher what was on the thumb drives for it to be of any use in taking down the Organization.

In the end, Claudia and Joe would spearhead the operation for finding all the information that had been downloaded from the Organization's computer, and the pertinent information would take weeks to figure out. Knowing this, the rest of the team left Claudia and Joe with the IT team to work on it, while they were off recovering from their early morning adventure.

With this portion of the job done, everybody went to their hotel rooms and slept until the next day, all agreeing they would be back the next morning ready to see and learn what was on the thumb drives and get ready for the next step in bringing down the Organization.

Chapter XVII

The next morning Buck and Rachael were in the IT shop, waiting for the rest of the team to make their entrance. Claudia and Joe were busy with the IT team, having already arrived. Both of them were in their element here and had been there an hour or two earlier, assisting in the download of information from the thumb drives. As everyone else started to show up, they all met in the IT shop to see if anything of value had been found on the hard drives.

When Lucas, Miguel and Mike showed up, the team was all there, waiting to hear some good news for their efforts of getting into the building. Claudia and Joe saw their teammates and smiled, giving the thumbs-up gesture to them.

Buck went up and asked Claudia and Joe, "Would it be easier to meet in the conference room, seeing as how it's standing-room only in here?"

"Give us five minutes and we'll meet you there," Claudia said.

As everybody shuffled out the door of the IT room, it gave the team a chance to get some more coffee and find a place to sit down and drink it. Everybody was still excited about getting in and out of the building yesterday and you could still feel the energy in the room. Claudia and Joe walked into the conference room and sat at the front of the conference table.

Race, who was sitting there, said, "Without further ado, here are Claudia and Joe."

Everybody clapped at the introduction and waited to hear from both of them. Joe looked at Claudia. "Ladies first."

"Thank you, Joe. Here is what we have found so far." Looking at her notes, she continued, "We found their main route for the drugs and arms shipments. We also found who is being bought off by the Organization and by how much. We found that they are working with the Russians and the old mafia in Italy as well."

"This is just the tip of the iceberg, so far," interrupted Joe as he sat there.

"We found their offshore bank accounts, as well as the money-laundering businesses they use," Claudia continued.

Joe couldn't contain himself anymore and jumped in. "It'll take weeks to get through all the information we downloaded onto the thumb drives."

Claudia shook her head in agreement with Joe's statement. "This is a treasure trove of information, and it also shows the other organizations they are affiliated with in their business dealings."

Race raised his hand, "When can we start acting on the information you've found?"

Joe and Claudia looked at each other for a second, trying to come up with a timeline, and as they were conversing with each other, Buck also asked, "When can we start hurting the Organization?"

"Well, that's not so easy to say at this point," said Joe.

"To do it right, it will take some time to figure out the best process for doing this without raising any suspicions," Claudia said.

"Can we start siphoning the money from one account and deposit it into the other bad guys' account?" asked Buck.

"Again, the answer is the same as before," said Joe. "We need to see the whole picture in order to hurt them the worst. If you can give us a week, we should be able to have some answers for you. In the meantime, we have their drug delivery schedules you can have for fun to mess with."

Mike, who had been quiet, looked over at Miguel and Lucas. "Oh boy, here's our chance to screw up the works for the Organization."

Both Lucas and Miguel's faces lit up with what Mike had said. "I can hardly wait to start," said Miguel.

"What we want is to photograph their drop-offs and money exchanges for a matter of record. That way, we not only get the buyers but the dealers, as well," said Race.

"Good point, Race. We need to catch them red-handed and have them turn on their bosses for lighter jail sentences for themselves. It will be the survival of the fittest and the fastest talking," Buck said.

"If we give you a week for deciphering the download from the hard drive, will that be enough to get the big picture?" Race asked Claudia and Joe.

Joe and Claudia looked at each other and nodded. "Should be, barring any unforeseen issues."

"Good, we'll leave you two to press on. If you'll give us the information on the drug deliveries, that should keep the rest of us busy for a while," Race said.

"Here is the schedule for the drug shipments and pickups. I knew you would want these while Claudia and I played with the rest of the computer downloads," Joe said as he handed out the paper depicting the schedules.

After Joe and Claudia excused themselves to go back to the IT section, Race and Buck, with the rest of the team, gathered around the table to look at the schedule Joe had given them. Buck walked up to the whiteboard as Rachael and Race read off the dates and places for the drug shipments and drop-offs. After ten minutes of writing on the whiteboard, they had the complete list of places and times. Dividing up the work according to location, the teams began choosing who would go where to photograph and videotape the drop-offs.

Miguel and Lucas would work with Mike, as previously agreed to. Buck and Rachael would work with Race as the second team to view and capture on film their assigned drug shipments and locations. When this was done, Mike's team would be the first to go out and photograph the transactions. Race's team would go out later in the evening the following night to go to their first assignment. Having the teams operating this way would not arouse any suspicions by the Organizations people. In the meantime, everybody on the other team took some personal time off to take care of their own needs and enjoy seeing the sights and sound of the city.

Buck and Rachael played tourists, visiting New York and Broadway and seeing the sights of the Statue of Liberty, Ellis Island, Empire State Building, and Central Park, all the while taking pictures for Marissa and the kids.

Mike, Lucas, and Miguel got set up for their first mission that afternoon, grabbing a camera and plenty of videotape to use. Mike was looking at the map of the area, trying to decide which location was best for watching the exchanges between the dealers and the customers and being able to film it. Short of being there and seeing it for themselves, this would have to be the best that they could do.

Arriving at the sight they had picked two hours earlier, they set up the camera in an abandoned warehouse building from across the street to record the drug transactions. From there, they could see and record who was driving in and out and the drug deals as they went down. The camera would be operated by Lucas, while Miguel and Mike would be watching everything go down from the other side of the building, closest to the corner where the drug dealers were. With Mike and Miguel in their location, hiding in the shadows of the building, from their vantage point they would give Lucas a heads up when the bad guys arrived. Now, it was a matter of being patient and waiting for them to show.

After about 30 minutes of waiting, the dealers arrived in their cars and were setting up their men in anticipation of the arrival of the suppliers. The dealer had his men take up places for security behind boxes and junk food machines to make sure the deal didn't go bad, with only the main dealer and one of his henchmen standing out in the open to be seen as they waited. As the other car pulled in and the men got out of their cars, they scanned the area, looking for anything out of the ordinary. Seeing nothing, the main supplier got out of his car and walked up to the other dealer, shaking his hand. Each of the men had a gym bag in their other hand. As the tradeoff started, each checked the other's gym bag to make sure everything was in order. The money exchange for the drug transaction was over in about five minutes, and each team got into their respective vehicles and left the warehouse. Going in different directions away from the warehouse, each group was gone in about five minutes. After waiting another ten minutes, Mike and Miguel met Lucas near the door of the warehouse. Lucas was excited to capture the deal on videotape and was showing it to Mike and Miguel. The first videotaping deal for the team became the benchmark for the rest of the team and the downfall of the Organization. In about a week they had all of the key players identified by facial recognition, having videotaped all of the transactions for the Organization. Everything was categorized according to location and time; the photographs taken were used for the clarity of the exchanges.

Buck, Rachael, and Race were able to record their transactions the same way. By the end of the week, the bulletin board was full of pictures of every player involved with the Organization at the lower levels. The next step was another meeting to learn what Joe and Claudia had found that would help shut down the money laundering side of the Organization permanently.

This meeting with Joe and Claudia would be the biggest meeting yet for the team; at least, Buck and Race hoped it would be. As they waited for Claudia and Joe to show up, they all sat there drinking their coffee and trying to guess which move they would make next. As they talked among themselves, Joe and Claudia came running up to the briefing room with a stack of papers in their hands. As Claudia started speaking, Joe handed out the briefing notes for them to follow. Lowering the movie screen, Joe loaded a thumb drive into the computer and got it set up for their presentation.

"Wow, you won't believe what we found in the stuff we downloaded from their computer," Claudia said excitedly.

Joe hit the enter key to show the first PowerPoint slide. On the slide, it showed the sphere of influence the Organization had all over Europe and America. Even Buck and Rachael were astounded by what they saw on the slide. Race didn't say a word as he sat there listening and watching the whole presentation. Mike, Lucas, and Miguel were amazed at how elaborate the Organization was and what they controlled. Some of the slides showed the amounts of money being transacted from one bank to another, with small businesses laundering the money before it hit the banks as deposits for the Organization. The slides showed which bank had what money in it and where the money was spent or used to get more drugs and people on both sides of the ocean.

The gangs were identified by their location and operations they performed for the Organization from all of the Latin American countries and inside the U.S. and Europe. The leaders of the gangs were identified, as well, and how much money they made working for the Organization. One of the slides showed future options as to where they wanted to expand and who their points of contact would be. When Claudia and Joe were done with the presentation, everybody just sat there trying to take it all in, yet not wanting to believe that the Organization was so vast and so well organized.

At this point, everybody took a ten minute break to collect their thoughts and to get more coffee. After settling down again, Race and Buck looked at Joe and Claudia, thanking them for their work and the briefing they gave.

Race spoke first to the group, "Wow, did we hit the mother lode or what?" Everybody chuckled at his comment, knowing exactly how he felt.

"Well, where do we start on tearing down the Organization and incarcerating the people in it?" asked Buck. He continued, "Remember, in our first meeting we talked about having the players turn on each other to start the ball rolling? Well, it has to start at the grass roots of the Organization. The dealers and the buyers are the first to fall. Then we work our way up to Danny the Jackal and nail him with everything we can find. The problem is, this organization is bigger than we thought at first, which means more players will be involved with the take down."

"How do we retain our secrecy of taking down the Organization with other players outside this room?" asked Race.

"Now you understand what I'm trying to say. According to the one slide, which showed who was being paid off and by how much, we know where we don't want to go for help," said Buck.

"How do you want to handle this one, Race?" asked Rachael.

"To be honest, I really don't know where to start on this. I think what Buck suggested is where we should start at the local level and we let The DEA and CIA and the other alphabets do their part."

"How about the U.S. Marshals getting involved with this? I recognize some of the people we filmed as being wanted by our agency," Mike said.

Looking at Claudia and Joe, Race asked, "Can you start funneling money from different accounts to set up the gangs for the fall?"

Joe smiled, "I thought you would never ask. Show them what we found, Claudia."

Claudia put up another slide, showing where they could touch their bank accounts and set up a trail showing how the gangs were holding back on the money being delivered to the Organization.

"These accounts are the most vulnerable that we have found, so far. We can even freeze some of the companies who are laundering the money for the Organization because they are on, or working for a company on American soil," Claudia said.

"Great, go ahead and start the process," said Race.

"Mike, I want you to go after the ones you recognize from the marshals' perspective," said Buck.

"Use Miguel and Lucas as U.S. Marshals as a cover for

right now. We don't want them thinking that there are other law-enforcement units involved just yet," Race said.

"Not a problem. I'll use some of our own men to go after these guys, as well. Maybe we can get them to turn on each other," Mike said.

"The main goal, as I see it, is to bring down Danny the Jackal with his men going under, as well.

"Race, do you want the other alphabets involved with our meetings from this point on?" asked Buck.

Race thought about this for a minute. "How much do we tell them and who would they report to, as far as progress goes?"

"How about we expand our operation to all the key units; that way we still control what happens on all levels of the operation, and that way we don't step on anybody's toes politically in the process," said Rachael.

"I like it. I'll check with Kennedy and see how he wants to handle it from here," Race said, continuing, "This looks like a full-blown operation for all of us to work on."

"Let's set up a meeting with Kennedy and run the PowerPoint presentation by him and we'll go from there," Buck said.

"I'll set it up. We'll need Claudia and Joe on this to give the briefing to Kennedy, in case there are any questions asked," Race said.

"Joe and Claudia nodded in agreement. "Not a

problem. We'll be there; just let us know when," said Joe.

"Okay, with that done, we'll need a plan of attack as to which bank accounts are being hit for holding money for the gangs," Race said.

Claudia looked up. "We can have that ready by this afternoon. Do you want us to start the paperwork to freeze the accounts we can touch, as well?"

"Yes, but don't do anything just yet. I'll need to run this by Kennedy but only after the meeting with him first," Race said.

Race looked at Buck and Rachael, "Can you guys run by yourselves for today while I get this other stuff done?"

"Oh sure, I see how it is; we do the work and you get to do the grip-and-grin with the high mucky-mucks," Buck said, smiling, continuing, "Better you than me, bud."

Race laughed, "There are days I would rather be busting down the doors, instead of knocking on them."

"Isn't that the truth," Rachael said.

"Oh, by the way, you're doing good, chief," Buck said.

The look on Race's face said it all without saying a word. By then, Buck and Rachael were on their way out of the building, headed to the prearranged drop-off to film the exchange of drugs and money. As both of them got into the car, they each looked at each other and smiled, "This is fun, I sure miss this part of the job," said

Rachael.

"Yeah, me to. Being stuck behind a desk isn't my idea of fun either," replied Buck.

Chapter XVIII

Buck and Rachael sat waiting with the camera in place, the drop-off point being an old garage in the middle of the worst-hit area of New Jersey. The lonely street in the old neighborhood was littered with trash as bad as you would see crossing the border into Tijuana, Mexico. The old cars were everywhere, some of them burned and others stripped and left sitting on blocks. This neighborhood was forgotten by humankind and left to die an agonizing death. People were still living here and you could see them peering through their windows at anybody new in the old neighborhood. To the locals, Buck and Rachael were the new items of curiosity for the area as they moved around inside the garage. Their vehicle was hidden from view of the dealers and buyers and could be seen from where Buck sat to make sure it didn't get stripped like the other cars sitting outside the warehouse.

After ten minutes of waiting, the first car showed up and the people got out, making sure they were alone. This time, the setup for security was different from the others they had witnessed. These men all had automatic weapons and they were set up in different corners of the first floor layout. Buck and Rachael were hiding on the second floor inside an office, watching through the broken glass of the door. The second car showed up about five minutes later. The people in that car got out and searched the room for the other guys' team. Buck looked at Rachael, "I got a bad feeling about this."

Hearing this, Rachael moved from the door to the stairwell and laid flat on the walkway, peering over the edge of the stairs, waiting to see what would happen next. Buck made sure the camera was running and focused on all of the key players. As usual, the two leaders met in the middle and started talking. The duffle bags held the money and the trunk of the second car was open. The driver of the second car pulled out a weapon and handed it to the gun dealer, who cocked it and let off a magazine load of bullets. The buyer took the gun and held it in his hands and lifted it to his shoulder and pointed it at an imaginary target across the warehouse. He was smiling at the one who gave him the gun. The gun dealer motioned for his man near the trunk to bring out the other guns and lay them out on the ground. Buck could see that there were three cases of these weapons, each case holding six automatic rifles. Buck recognized them as M-27 infantry automatic rifles that were known for being light weight, magazine fed and were used by the Marine Corp. Rachael, who was watching from the stairwell, saw a shadow move across the floor, getting closer to the leader and his men of the second car. In a minute, the shadow raised his weapon and started firing at the men from the second car. After the first shot was fired, the other men who were hiding joined in, and in about 30 seconds everybody from the second car, including the gun dealer, lay on the ground, dead or dying. The buyer, from the first car, had his men load the guns and the duffle bag full of money into the trunk of his car. After the car left, Rachael crawled back to where Buck was kneeling by the door. "What do we do now?"

"Not to worry, we got it all on tape, including the license plate of the car and clear pictures of the gunmen that did the shooting."

Going downstairs after taking down the video camera, Buck and Rachael took pictures of the dead guys for the computer geeks to do a facial recognition on later. As Rachael was taking the pictures, one of the men moved, startling Rachael. She jumped back, calling for Buck to come over. Buck rushed over to where Rachael was standing, "What's wrong?"

"This guy is still alive."

Kneeling over him to check his breathing, Buck called 911 to get an ambulance to the scene. After the ambulance came, the EMTs worked on the man to get him stable enough to drive to the hospital. Rachael rode in the ambulance while Buck drove their car, following the ambulance to the hospital. Waiting at the hospital for the doctor's report, Rachael called Race. "We just witnessed a hit go down on a bad arms deal; what do you want us to do?"

"Are there any survivors?"

"One man survived the shooting, but we don't know if he'll live yet. We're waiting for the doctor now. One more thing, we got it all on camera."

"Good news, then. I'll call the local police and let them know what went down and that we got it covered from our end. When do you expect to be back?"

"As soon as we hear from the doctors in the emergency room, who are operating on the guy right now; he's in pretty bad shape."

"Good. I'll see you when you get here."

Buck and Rachael stayed at the hospital, waiting almost two hours to talk to the doctors about their patient. The doctor came out and, seeing Buck and Rachael standing there, walked over to them. "Are you the two that found the guy we just worked on?"

"Yes, we are," Buck replied.

"Well, I'm surprised the guy got through the operation without dying on the table. He has a strong will to live. He lost a lot of blood but I think he'll survive if he can get through the night."

"Can we talk to him right now?" Buck asked.

"He's pretty sedated right now. I would wait a couple of days before questioning him about anything."

"All right, that's what we'll do then, and thank you for saving him," Buck said.

"I didn't save him; he has a strong will to survive, that's all. I wish all of my patients had that kind of will to survive."

Buck looked at Rachael, "You know, if the bad guys who did this find that one of the men they shot survived, they'll want to come back and finish the job before he talks."

"Are you implying one of us should stay here and babysit this guy?"

"'Bout sums it up for me. If you wish, I'll stay and you get back to the office with the video and make sure Race gets the tape."

Rachael started to leave. "I'll let Race know we have a witness that survived and may be able to turn him on the ones that did this to him."

Buck nodded, "When you come back, bring me some coffee, will you?"

As Rachael walked away hearing his request, she raised her hand and waved at him to acknowledge what he said.

Buck walked over to the nurses' station to find out what room the man would be put in, then headed in that direction to wait for him to come back from post-surgery. The man was wheeled in about an hour later, still unconscious.

Rachael reported to Race, "Buck decided to babysit the man at the hospital, just in case somebody came back to finish the job."

Race picked up the phone at his desk and called Kennedy. "We need to send two men to guard the man at the hospital where Buck is."

Thirty minutes later, Buck was back at the office, sitting next to Rachael, drinking coffee. They were both waiting to see if Race had any more information from the videotape of the arms deal.

After watching the videotape, Race said, "You did good to get this on tape. What we need now is to know who the people are that did the hit."

"They're not part of the Organization?" Rachael asked.

"No, they're not. The fact is, we think it's a new player trying to take over the business, or so it appears."

"Do you have any ideas as to who it is?" Buck asked.

"Not at this time, we don't. Maybe we need to bring the team back together to figure this out."

"I believe you're right on doing that," Buck replied.

Race made the phone calls to the other team members. "We need to meet again; something new has come up."

Later that afternoon, the team was assembled in the conference room, seated and waiting for Race and Buck to appear in order to start.

Race and Buck showed up and turned on the videotape of the arms deal that had gone bad. Everybody sat there, watching and waiting for the next part of the briefing to start.

"Does anybody recognize the players in this video?" Race asked.

"The arms dealer is Chucky the Clown and is known as a sadistic little S.O.B., known for acting like a clown when he is with his friends," Mike said. "The others, I don't know about."

"We think they may be new players on the field. I've checked all of my sources and nobody can identify them," said Race.

"We're not sure how much of a part they play in the Organization's business yet. What has been done as far as siphoning the money out of the accounts and putting it into the gang's bank accounts?" asked Buck.

Joe and Claudia answered the question. "We've already started the process and slowly the money is being taken out and set up in another bank account on one of the Treasure Island banks. So far, they have 500,000 dollars in the account."

"Mike, do you have anything to report on your efforts on the drug deals?" Race asked.

"We've videotaped about six meetings, so far, nothing to write home about, as far as being other than normal stuff."

"Then, I take it that it's so far, so good. Just to let you know, the DEA said thank you for the information we gave them from the hard drive downloads. For them, it filled in a lot of gaps in their Intel makeup of the dealers and runners," Race said.

"Do you think it would be a good time to start freezing their accounts, now?" Buck asked.

"I'm not sure; let's wait a little longer for the impact to be more effective. Oh, one more thing, we got a survivor of the arms deal and we're waiting to talk to him about what he knows," Race replied, talking to the others in the group.

"What do you want us to do now?" Mike asked.

Buck jumped in at this point, "Begging your pardon, Race, how about we go after the dealers on the street now?"

"Anything to bring Danny out into the open, is that what you're thinking?" Race asked.

"Yes, sir, it's exactly what I'm thinking, Race."

"Be my guest, and all of his people, too; and, by the way, happy hunting."

All of the team members were smiling now that they would be able to actually bust the bad guys and bring them in. It was one thing to observe their activities but it's another to be able to arrest them for it.

Chapter XIX

The next morning, Mike, Miguel, and Lucas, drove their car to where the dealers worked the corner of the street. Waiting in the car just inside one of the side alleys, Mike watched the street corner for any signs of life. Lucas and Miguel had positioned themselves in the shadows between the apartment houses, watching and waiting, as well. When the first dealer showed up, Mike drove up to the corner, asking to buy some crack from the dealer. When the dealer went to his supplier, he came back with a baggie full of crack. When the dealer stuck his head into the car to get the money, Lucas put a gun to his head, "You're under arrest for selling."

The dealer tried to jump back out of the car window, but Mike grabbed him by the hair and held him till Lucas could put cuffs on him. The supplier saw what was happening and pulled out his gun to shoot Luca. Miguel, seeing this, yelled, "Now don't do anything stupid, you hear me!"

Lucas, hearing Miguel yelling at the supplier, quickly turned around with the dealer in front of him. As the supplier fired his gun, it hit the dealer in the chest, at which time Miguel fired and hit the supplier in the leg. By now, the whole neighborhood was awakened by the gunfire. Lucas and Miguel jumped into the car and drove away as fast as they could out of the neighborhood.

Mike looked at the two of them, laughing about what had happened on the street corner. Mike shook his head, "Man, you guys are crazy, aren't you?"

"So, where is the next place we're going to?" Lucas asked, smiling.

"They're doing a drug drop off for money in about two hours. How about we go pay them a visit," Mike said.

"Let's call Buck and Rachael in on this one, too," said Miguel. "That way, we get the money and the drugs this time."

With Buck, Rachael, and Race in place at the drop off point near the opening of the door of the building and Mike and company on the other side and in place inside the building, the team waited for the transaction to take place. The first car came into the building and, as usual, they set the security inside and around the boss. Miguel and Lucas went to where their security people were and disabled them, taking their guns and zip-tying the guards' hands and feet after gaging them. Once this was completed, Mike, Miguel, and Lucas took their place as the security team. Lucas started making his way to the car, pulling his knife out, he stuck one of the tires of the car and watched the leader, hoping the noise wouldn't attract him.

Waiting for the second car to show, Buck and Race hid themselves behind some boxes near the front of the building. Then, as the car drove through the opening, Buck and Race made their move, sneaking up behind the car. Buck took a loading strap and hooked the door handle on one side of the car and rolled it under the car to the other side with Race hooking the other door handle, cinching it tight, so that the security team couldn't get out of the car. The leader of the second car got out and, realizing he and the front passenger were the only ones able to get out of the car, just stood there. The other leader pulled his gun and started looking around to see what was going on.

By now, Miguel was pointing his gun at the leader of the first car, ordering the man to lay his gun down. The second guard from the first car saw Miguel and Lucas standing there with their guns pointed at him and dropped his gun to the floor. The second car's leader and security did the same. Race called 911 and asked that the police show up at the address he had given them. With both cars with flat tires sitting inside the building and the drugs on one car hood and the money sitting on the other car hood, everybody waited for the police to show up. The men in the second car had already thrown out their weapons and were just sitting in the car when the cops arrived. When the police got there, it was just them and the two cars with the money and the drugs out in the open. The police came in and arrested the men in the car, as well as the men that were tied up leaning up against the car.

The cops looked around, trying to figure out what had happened. Not knowing who phoned in the call, they took the money and the drugs and hauled them away for processing, with the credit going to the police department for catching the bad guys and getting the money and drugs off the streets.

Danny the Jackal, reading the newspaper about how the police found the drugs and money at the warehouse, was furious that his men had got caught in the deal. The papers said it was about half a million dollars that was found in the duffle bag, and the drugs that were confiscated were the biggest catch of the police precinct's history. Fifty kilos of crack were confiscated in the raid. The paper said some good Samaritan called it in and the police showed up with no one there, except the bad guys with the drugs and money.

Danny the Jackal was trying to figure out what had happened and how it could have even occurred. He started making calls trying to find out who was doing this to him. His seconds in command were all trying to find the answers for their boss. The word on the street was that somebody tried to arrest a dealer and in the process the dealer was shot and killed by his own supplier. The question still remained, who was involved in this and what were they trying to do?

Race was just sitting there, happy not to have to fill out the paperwork for the bust. Mike and company laughed at the looks on the faces of the men in each car as the camera crew from the local news filmed it. Buck and Rachael were chuckling, as was Race, for catching the two cars of men, drugs and the money, to boot.

The money confiscated would be used by the police department, once it was cleared for use on new equipment for the precinct. The drugs would be destroyed by the feds in the near future after the court case was over. The men, if they were smart, would start talking to the narcotics detectives to get lighter sentences for themselves by telling who they worked for and where they were. All in all, a good day's work for everyone, with more coming down the road, compliments of the downloaded hard drives.

As the seconds in command were searching to find out who it was that let it out about the drug drop-off, they started talking to the bookkeeper who managed the bank accounts for the Organization. Knowing something was wrong with the numbers in the accounts, they took the bookkeeper to Danny. "We think we have a problem in our record-keeping area."

"I found some irregularities in the numbers in our Treasure Island bank accounts," said the bookkeeper.

"What do you mean, irregularities?" Danny asked.

"Well, from the looks of it, we're half a million short in one of our accounts and more is being taken out each day. There is a new account set up in the bank by one of the gang leaders that works for us. Our informant told me this when I called him to find out if there was a discrepancy in our records."

Danny stopped for a minute and, thinking out loud, said, "Why would they be trying to steal from me when we have been doing business for so long with no problems? We need to meet the gang leader about this now, right now!" Danny said angrily.

"Yes, sir, I'll set up the meeting for today at three o'clock at the usual place," one of the seconds in charge said.

The gang leader, when hearing about needing to meet with Danny, was surprised by the request and, of course, agreed to the meeting. Not knowing why, he started thinking about the drug deal that went bad and also one of his dealers being shot by his own supplier. He said to one of his enforcers, "We need to be ready for anything to happen."

The enforcer had all his people ready for the meeting at two o'clock. The usual place was in the old part of town by the water docks, where you could see the New York skyline in the distance. At the prearranged time and place, all the players were there. Danny drove up in his SUV and the gang leader drove up in his Cadillac. Each man stepped out of his vehicle, watching and waiting for the other to make a move. They met in the middle between the vehicles, standing about three feet apart. Danny spoke first, "What's this I hear about losing my drugs and money to the cops?"

"Man, I don't know what you're talking about. We had nothing to do with that at all."

"Can you explain to me about a new bank account with half a million dollars of my money in it, which is in your name?"

The gang leader was surprised by the accusation from Danny. "What are you talking about? We didn't take your money and I don't have an account at any bank anywhere."

"Then explain this," Danny said, holding out the paperwork to the gang leader, who grabbed it and started looking at it. The gang leader recognized the paperwork as bank statements and couldn't believe what he was seeing.

He looked at Danny, "I had nothing to do with this; you got to believe me that I'm telling the truth!"

Danny pulled out his gun and shot the gang leader in the head and smiled, "I believe you now."

When the gang leader hit the ground, the gang leader's henchmen, who were hiding, opened fire on Danny's enforcers, taking two of them down. Danny ran to get back into his SUV and drove out of there as quickly as he could go, leaving his enforcers to fight it out with the gang henchmen. When the smoke cleared, both sides had taken hits; but the gang ended up winning the battle.

Danny was furious with what had happened to his men, as well as the 500,000 dollars missing from his bank accounts. He knew that he had to act fast or the gang would literally take over the Organization. Getting on his cell phone, he called some of his other men. "We need to take out the gang of dealers and set up a new group to run it."

The voice on the other end said, "No problem. We'll take care of it for you."

"Good. Let me know when it is done. Goodbye."

As he closed his cell phone, his mind was going through all the steps necessary to rebuild his distribution network and what it would take to get it working again. For the first time, he was concerned that he was losing control of his Organization and that it might be failing. Danny the Jackal wasn't laughing anymore, especially with losing half a million dollars due to some punk gang members getting greedy.

Danny's team of thugs were in position to take out the gang who stepped on Danny's toes. Each gang member would not see tomorrow. As each gang member was approached to buy drugs from Danny's men, they would kill the gang member that worked as a dealer. By the time it was all done, the gang members were afraid to leave their houses, for fear that Danny's guys were waiting for them. In one day, all of the drug distribution network was gone and the gang was decimated by the Organization's henchmen, with new people stepping in to take over the street corner to sell the drugs.

Joe and Claudia had siphoned the money from the Organization placing it in the accounts of the other players in the Organization, especially the groups in Latin America. Danny was watching his whole distribution system starting to fail and didn't understand why it was happening. Why would anybody want to cross him, when everything had been working fine before? He started thinking that somebody else was playing or maybe trying to take over the Organization outright. As he thought about this, he started wondering who was powerful enough to try this.

Unbeknownst to Danny, his key suppliers from Latin America wouldn't be able to supply his drugs because of the DEA stepping in and arresting the growers and suppliers before the drugs left to come to America. The CIA had already tracked the money from the accounts on the Treasure Islands to Europe and was starting to freeze the assets of the banks in Europe that were involved with the drug money. The laundering businesses had already been identified and were being watched and couldn't move a dollar without the feds knowing it.

The money trail was on the verge of drying up, and without the money the Organization was hemorrhaging badly. Interpol was stepping in, as was every major police agency in Europe, and building up evidence to bring charges against the banking establishments and the key members in each bank for conspiring to distribute drug money for the Organization.

The Latin American countries were being watched, as well, not only by the Americans but by the police organizations on the islands themselves. The wheels of justice were poised and ready to take down the Organization from top to bottom.

A team set up by the FBI was watching the turf war going on in New Jersey and all along the Eastern Seaboard of the United States. Danny's men were very good at taking down the gang members as they went from city to city. The war between the Organization and the gang was being fought in the streets of the American cities. It was nothing unusual to hear about a gangland shootout on the corners of where the drug dealers were peddling their drugs. The other gangs, seeing this, would try to take over the drug business by wiping out the gang who once had protection from the Organization.

Mike and company would go into a certain city and would disrupt the drug deal going down and let the existing police department confiscate the drugs and money and the gang members, as well. Danny couldn't believe all of this was happening to his network. The key players were somehow disappearing and couldn't be found anywhere. The justice system was methodically removing the players one by one.

Buck, Rachael, and Race, would go to the banks with warrants and arrest the bankers involved with the money laundering for the bank and have them turn states witnesses against other players inside the Organization; specifically, the businesses involved with laundering and then turning the money over to the banks. Buck, Rachael, and Race, would go into the businesses and with court orders and warrants shut them down. Interpol and other European agencies were doing the same all over Europe, including Russia and Italy.

In just a matter of days, the Organization was brought to its knees and Danny couldn't understand why it was happening. He was losing control of the Organization and was starting to run scared. With all the other police departments cracking down on the Organization's drug empire, Mike and company, as well as Buck, Rachael and Race, headed back to New Jersey and started putting together all of the warrants to pick up the rest of the players still standing within the Organization.

It was only a matter of time before the Organization would fall. For Buck and Rachael, it was about finding where Danny was hiding now and flushing him out of the woodwork. By the second month, Mike and company were back in the office and were running all of their operations against the Organization from there. Race no longer needed to be out in the field; he was busy coordinating all the warrants and pickups of the members by the other DEA, U.S. Marshals and Interpol offices. He left the searching for Danny to Buck, Rachael, Miguel, and Lucas. With one more job still open from the arms deal, Buck and Rachael decided it was time to interview the lone survivor of the arms deal that went bad.

Rachael and Buck, working with Miguel and Lucas, went to the hospital where the lone survivor was recuperating from being shot. They had Miguel and Lucas stay in the waiting room while they talked to the lone survivor. Buck and Rachael went to his room, meeting the two FBI agents who were guarding the door. They let Buck and Rachael pass through the hospital room door. Sitting down next to the man, Buck introduced himself and Rachael as agents working for the FBI and also the ones who saved his life after the arms deal went bad.

At first, when the lone survivor realized they were FBI agents, he clammed up and wouldn't say a word, telling them to leave. Once he realized they had saved his life, his attitude changed. "I owe you my life, and because of that I'll tell you what you want to know."

"We would like to know who it was that put you here," Buck said.

"I really don't know who they were, except they were new kids on the block, wanting to get involved with everything that they could make money on."

"Anything else you can think of?"

"All I know is that they came from El Salvador and they play pretty mean, even with their own people."

"Do you have any idea where they stay at?"

"No, not really; like I said, I was low man on the pole when it came to decisions being made."

"One more time, do you have any idea who they were working for?"

"The impression I get is that they're working for themselves, trying to build up their presence in the city."

"All right. Get well and be careful out there."

"Yeah, I will, and thanks for saving my life."

"You're very welcome."

Buck and Rachael met Miguel and Lucas in the waiting room, where they sat down and told them of their conversation with the lone survivor. As Miguel and Lucas listened to their answers, trying to figure out their next move, Lucas said, "How about we check with Mike on this; he has so many connections out there. I'm sure he would know where to look for the guns."

"Good idea," Rachael said.

When they got back to the office, Mike was sitting in the break room, sorting out the warrants he had been given by Race. Looking at him, you could tell he didn't like this part of the job.

Buck walked up to him, "Would you like to have some fun, instead of doing that?"

"Anything is better than this stuff."

"Don't you have any others that can do that for you?" asked Lucas.

"As a matter of fact, I do; let me make a phone call and I'll be with you in a minute." At that point, Mike got up and walked into the office to make a call.

A little while later, Mike came back to the break room smiling, "I'll let the rookie marshal do the grunt work for me today."

"Good. Let's go," Buck said.

With that, the team went out the door of the break room, back out onto the parking lot. "Mike, do you know where the El Salvadorans are staying in the city?" asked Buck.

"Why, yes, I do, why do you ask?"

"We believe they were the ones that blew the arms deal; leastwise, that's what the lone survivor said when we visited him at the hospital today."

"You don't say. Well, we've been after these guys for quite a while for just about everything we can think of."

"We don't have a warrant for this, and I'm not sure we could get one, either, but we need to get those guns off the streets."

"And your point is?" Mike said, smiling. "When do we go get them back?"

"How about right now; would that work for you?"

"Oh, you know how to say the right things, don't you?"

"That was way too easy," Buck smiled.

"Call me easy; however, I'm not cheap."

After giving Buck and Miguel the directions, the team piled into two cars to go to their destination in Asbury Park. Already starting to decline in population, from small to smaller, it had a bad reputation for gangs and murder and such. Parking their cars in an alleyway, the team got out and made their way to the street. Staying in the shadows so as not to be seen, Mike explained to them, "Once we leave this alley they'll know we're here, if they don't already know now. Let's wait until it's darker and then go in; that way our chances of getting out alive are better."

Buck agreed, as did the others, with Mike's suggestion. Fortunately, Lucas and Miguel had bought some candy bars before leaving the Federal Building. At seven o'clock pm, it was dark enough to move around without being seen for the most part. The locals were still active but blending in was easier now. Moving from the alleyway into the shadows of the night all dealt with timing. Walking with the crowd without being seen by the crowd was kind of hard at first, but moving without being seen was easier in the dark. After Mike and Lucas were in place by the main street building, Miguel and Buck made their way to the back of the building, waiting for a signal from the front. Rachael was the bait in this adventure, and as she started walking down the street, the men in front of the building noticed that she wasn't from around the neighborhood. They started making catcalls and coming up to her, trying to be macho. She blew all of them off by continuing to walk down the street.

When she got in front of the house, she stopped and asked one of the Salvadorans directions about where to buy a gun. The men looked at her, thinking she was a cop, pulled their guns on her. Mike and Lucas raised their guns and told the guys to drop theirs right now on the ground. By now, Rachael had her gun out, as well, and smacked the first guy that was mouthing off to her as she was walking down the street. Laying him out on the ground, the others dropped their weapons on cue. Forcing one of the men into the house and upstairs to the main room, they made their way into the front room, where the men sitting on the couch watching TV were caught totally by surprise. As they raised their own guns, Rachael shot the first one in the leg and watched as he fell to the ground holding his leg. By then, Mike and Lucas were in the front room, searching all the rooms on the first floor of the house. Finding nothing in the other rooms, they went to the guys sitting on the couch. "You guys steal some guns from an arms dealer about a week ago?

"What's it to you if we did?" asked one of the guys sitting on the couch.

With that answer, Lucas shot the guy in the leg, as well, and let him fall to the ground as he yelled in pain. Lucas pointed the gun at his head, "Shall we try this again?"

This time the man answered, "Yeah, man, we ripped the man off and killed all of his people standing there with him."

"Where are the guns now?" asked Mike.

"Man, we still got them downstairs in the basement."

By now, Miguel and Buck came through the back door of the building and were standing there watching the two men bleeding on the ground. Buck and Miguel offered to go down into the basement to get the guns. Grabbing one of the bleeders, they dragged him over to the door of the basement and had him open it. Just as he opened the door, shots rang out, hitting the bleeder in the chest. He fell forward down the stairs into the man that had fired the shots. Buck dispatched him with one round to the head, and waiting a minute longer, they grabbed the other bleeder and dragged him over to the basement door.

Buck looked at him, "You first, friend."

The bleeder went down the stairs with Buck hanging onto him as a shield to keep from being shot. The bleeder turned on the main light in the basement and pointed in the direction of the wooden boxes sitting on the floor. Buck grabbed the bleeder and pushed him over to the where the boxes were. "Open them, please."

The bleeder went over and opened the boxes and stepped back away from them, waiting to see what would happen to him. Miguel came down the stairwell and, keeping his gun on the bleeder, walked over to the boxes and looked inside. Miguel's eyes got wide as he was looking at two RPGs in one box, 50 hand grenades in the second box, and six MK-27s in the third box. The smaller boxes had three thousand rounds of ammunition for the MK-27s.

"What do we do with all of this now?" Miguel asked.

"There are two options here; they are, one, taking it from them or, two, blow it up here and the house, too. Which do you prefer to do?"

"Hold that thought for a moment while I ask the others."

In a few minutes, Miguel came back down, "It's our call for what we want to do."

"What should we do with the people? Should we bring them down here for when we blow up the building?" asked Buck, winking at Miguel and smiling.

The bleeder's eyes got big on that suggestion, and he started begging for his life right there. Miguel smiled. "Nah, it would be a waste of the building with them in it."

"Well, how about we destroy the guns using the hand grenades they have here, with everybody watching from outside the building."

"I like that idea. Let's do it."

As the rest of the team led the people out of the building and had them stand across the street to watch the explosion, Mike and Lucas opened the gas lines for the stove and heaters in the building. Bringing all the boxes up the stairs to the first floor, they stepped out of the front door and threw a match into the house. The initial explosion was from the gas inside the building. The other smaller explosions that followed were from the ammunition in the boxes going off.

In a matter of minutes, the building was totally engulfed in flames and the fire department was on their way to put out the fire. When they arrived, they were told about the ammunition inside the building and the hand grenades, as well. The fire department moved their trucks a quarter mile away from the fire and just stood there watching the building burn to the ground. Occasionally, you could hear sporadic ammunition going off from inside the fire.

After watching the house burn to the ground with the fire department, the team went back to their cars and drove off, leaving the fire department to save the surrounding buildings. The gang had nowhere to go and therefore disappeared into the night like cockroaches fleeing from the light, fearing that if they said anything they would be arrested.

The following week was a blur for the team. They were involved in a coordinated strike with the other alphabets as the warrants were served, bank accounts were frozen, and people were picked up and arrested for their part in the Organization's operations. At the end of the last day of the strike, everybody went to their lodgings and slept till Monday morning.

Arriving back at the FBI headquarters on Monday, the team reassembled once more in the conference room, getting ready for another briefing. This time Kennedy was there, as was Race standing next to him. The first five minutes was thanking the team for their hard work and determination not to falter in their duties, as far as being brought together to make a special team with the goal of destroying the Organization. Then the numbers and hard facts were put up on a slide to show what their work had accomplished.

Race addressed what was up on the slide, "In a short period of time...

1. One hundred fifty people were arrested for being involved in all levels of the organization inside the U.S.

2. Four banks here in the U.S. have closed their doors forever from paying the fines for money laundering.

3. At least 10 businesses were shut down and their accounts frozen by the local governments in their own countries.

4. The gangs that supplied and delivered the drugs to the U.S. and Europe were incarcerated and locked up in their countries' prisons.

5. The money that was frozen in the banks and the fines were given to the local police departments to assist in the drug wars.

6. Several politicians were forced to retire from office because of their affiliation with the Organization.

7. Danny the Jackal, the leader of the organization, has not been apprehended as of yet."

As a parting shot, Race and the team were given a standing ovation for their part in taking down a major player in the drug world.

After the meeting was complete, Buck and Rachael met with Race, shaking hands. Race spoke first, "Thank you for giving me a chance to prove myself to you and the rest of the team."

"You did this all on your own; you know, you remind of a young man I used to know a long time ago. He was the same way you were when he first started as a deputy in a small county in Arizona, full of fire and ready to take on the world. Fortunately, with the help of a few mentors, he turned into quite a cop. In fact, the rumor is, he became the sheriff of the county. You did well, and I'm proud of you for it," Buck replied.

All the while Buck was speaking, Rachael kept pointing at Buck behind his back so that Race could see it.

"Thank you, again, for all that you have done here. Oh, by the way, do you know anything about a fire in the worst part of New Jersey, where supposedly they found weapons and such?" Race asked.

"Wow, look at the time; we need to get back to our lodging at McGuire AFB to head out tomorrow," Buck said as he quickly left the room with Rachael in tow.

Race was laughing at how fast Buck and Rachael left

the room to go home.   As Buck and Rachael were leaving the building, Rachael received a phone call from Evans. "Our informants tell us the rumor is that Danny is hiding out at a restaurant in the Golden Nugget Hotel and Casino in Atlantic City and has been there for days, hiding out in public sight, staying at the hotel. Look for a guy wearing a flower in his lapel at the restaurant."

"Thanks, Evans, we'll let you know how it turns out," Rachael said.

She told Buck about what Evans had said. He went for the car and Rachael headed back into the building to get Lucas and Miguel.

Rachael, looking for Miguel and Lucas, told them of the phone call about Danny. They quickly came out of the building, getting into the car waiting for them. Buck and the team drove to Atlantic City to the Golden Nugget parking lot.

After walking around the casino for a while, Buck and Rachael went into the restaurant inside the casino and started looking for the man with a flower in his lapel. Finding him sitting in the corner, he nudged Rachael and headed in the direction of the man. Rachael was watching everything that went on as Buck walked up to the man.

Buck, sat down next to the man, "You know Evans?"

"Why, yes, I do," said the man. "He said there would be some people interested in knowing about a certain gentleman here at the hotel, is that true?"

"How would you ever guess that?"

"Just lucky, I suppose. The man you want is in room 314 and hasn't left it, except to come down and eat."

"I have to ask, why are you helping us?"

"The man killed my brother a while back, just for fun. Is that a good enough reason?"

"Works for me."

After walking away, Rachael continued watching the man until Buck was clear of him. Rachael, leaving with Buck, left the restaurant with Lucas and Miguel following them.

Reaching the third floor in the hotel, Lucas noticed that a waiter was bringing a cart of food down the hall. Lucas commandeered the food cart and the waiter's jacket, saying to the waiter, "I promise you'll get it back later when I'm done," slipping the waiter a 20 dollar bill for letting him borrow the coat and food tray.

Knocking on the door to room 314, Lucas yelled, "Room service." In a minute, the door opened and Lucas was let in with the food tray. Inside the room, along with Danny, were a couple of women just lounging around watching TV.

"Where would you like me to put the food tray, sir?" Lucas asked.

"Put it over by the window," Danny said, giving a 20 dollar tip to Lucas. Taking the tip and thanking him for it, Lucas walked out.

Once outside the room, Lucas returned the coat to the

waiter and reported to Buck and Rachael that it was indeed Danny in the room.

Miguel looked at Buck, "I want first shot at this guy."

Buck nodded in agreement. "We need to find a way to draw him out of his room."

Lucas started laughing out loud. "I got an idea. You, Buck, need to act drunk and start pounding on his door, pretending you can't get into your room." Buck smiled and, nodding his head, unbuttoned his shirt and messed up his hair.

"Now I know who you are," Rachael laughed.

Buck looked at her and smiled sarcastically. "Do you really want to go down this road?"

Buck headed down to the room and was singing and yelling and hitting the wall as he staggered down the hall, with Miguel following him, trying to get him to the right room in the hotel. Stopping at Danny's room, he pounded on the door, yelling for the little woman to open the door for a great big kiss. The first time he pounded on the door, Danny didn't open the door, figuring it was a drunk at the wrong room. The second time, Buck started pounding on the door, yelling, "Do you have a boyfriend in there, you flirt!?"

This time, Danny opened the door, ready to punch the drunk for being a jerk. Miguel was very apologetic about how Buck was acting, saying that he was trying to get him to his own room. Buck lunged at the door of the room, yelling, "Hey, little woman, show your face and quit hiding your boyfriend in the closet!"

At this point, Danny started getting mad and Miguel tried calming him down. And when he wasn't looking, Miguel sucker-punched him right between the eyes. Danny went to his knees and Buck grabbed him by the neck and pushed him down to the floor. The women in the room were told to leave or they would be going to jail, as well. Quickly getting dressed, they left the room in a real hurry. While Danny lay on the floor he was handcuffed and then put into a chair.

Miguel looked at him, "Do you know who I am?"

"No, I don't know who you are. But if you want money, I'll give you all I got to let me go," Danny said, pleading his case.

"I'm Miguel, and you put out a hit on me and my family in Phoenix a month or two back, using Vincent and Joey as the hitmen. You know those guys?"

Danny nodded, "It was nothing personal, I tell you, nothing personal at all."

Miguel hit him again, "It was personal to me. You understand that, Danny? And, by the way, I would like you to meet the other targets that your hitmen were to take out, as well."

Buck introduced himself and Rachael to Danny. "Have you figured out who destroyed your Organization yet?"

Danny looked at Buck and Rachael and cussed them for what they had done to his empire.

Buck continued, "I just want you to know that it was us that brought you down from your perch. You remember the problem you had with your sewage system backing up?"

Danny nodded yes.

"You guessed right, it was us that did that. I just wanted you to know who did it and why we did it," Buck said.

"Shall we call the police and lock him up?" asked Lucas.

"Yeah, maybe it's time for him to go now. You know, I would really like to blow his brains out right here and now," said Miguel.

Danny looked nervous after hearing Miguel say that. "You can't kill me in cold blood; that's against the law," Danny pleaded.

"How about we take him to the top of the hotel and throw him off the roof? That way everybody will think it's a suicide," Lucas said, smiling.

Danny was starting to sweat now and wasn't sure if they were kidding or not. By now, Danny was willing to do anything to stay alive. "I know the names of people that you could put away for a long time for other murders, drugs, and arms dealing. All you got to do is just ask, and I'll tell you."

"Maybe he might be worth more to us alive than dead," Rachael said.

"You know I am," said Danny, emphatically.

"I don't know. I kind of like the idea of throwing him off the roof," Buck said.

Miguel started to pick him up and take him to the sliding glass door in the room. By now, Danny was crying. "Please let me live. I'll tell you everything I know about other organizations I've worked with."

Rachael and Lucas grabbed Danny and sat him back down in the chair. Miguel walked outside into the hallway with Buck. "Are you ready to turn him over to the FBI?"

"I think he's ready to go now. I think he'll need a change of clothes when he gets where he is going," Buck said, laughing with Miguel.

Later that evening, the FBI office was called out to come and pick up Danny the Jackal in his briefs. As they paraded him in front of the gambling crowd, everybody stopped for moment and watched as he was loaded into a car in front of the hotel.

Race was one of the arresting agents for the FBI and was surprised that Danny was still in one piece, considering all that he was responsible for when it came to Miguel and Buck. Again shaking Buck's hand, Race said, "I guess this means it's over for you guys."

"Yep, it's over for us now. We can go home and get back to our own lives again. I've still have one more stop before going home," Buck said.

"We have some kids who are wondering if their parents are ever coming home again," Rachael said.

The next day, sitting at the airport in Philadelphia, Buck and Rachael, along with Miguel and Lucas, were waiting for the airline agent at the counter to allow boarding for the flight home to Phoenix. The flight was long, but finally touching down in Phoenix everybody breathed a sigh of relief. Their adventure, or ordeal, depending on how you looked at it, was over for the time being. Arriving home, Miguel gave Marissa a great big hug, and the kids were jumping up and down and hugging Miguel and wouldn't let go of him for quite a while. Rachael hugged her children, as did Buck, who were disappointed when they had to leave after a few days to go home.

Buck called Foster to check in on him and Elaine and, finding all was good, relayed the news. "The Organization has been taken apart and Danny the Jackal is finally behind bars."

"You still need to go on a fishing trip with me, you know."

"It's a deal, name the time and we'll be there come hell or high water."

"Fair enough, and we'll let you know when."

Before leaving to go back home, Buck and Miguel made a trip up to Vegas to check in with Evans and Linda and let them know the results of the take down of the Organization and its impact for all concerned. Evans and Linda listened to all the stories and were laughing about how Danny was caught by a drunk in his hotel room. For all concerned, there was only one thing left to do, and that was to go visit Frankie in prison.

Arriving at the prison, the guard went and told Frankie he had visitors waiting to see him. Frankie was feeling pretty good, thinking that Buck and Rachael and their families were dead. When he showed up in the meeting room, he met at a table with Evans and Linda first. Frankie, looking pretty happy, was told by Evans and Linda that Buck and Rachael were gone, along with their stepson and his family. Frankie started laughing and feeling pretty good about it. Then, Buck and Miguel stood up and walked over to where Frankie was. Doing a double take, looking at Buck and Miguel, he stopped smiling. Buck reached down and handed Frankie a small package. "I thought you might like having these for your souvenirs."

"What are these rings from?"

"This ring is from Vincent and the other ring is from Joey. I took them off their dead bodies after we killed them," Buck said.

"And here is a picture of Danny leaving one of the hotels in New Jersey, compliments of the FBI. You can keep that, if you want, for the wall in your cell," Buck added, smiling.

"One other thing, just so you know, you are being charged with three counts of attempted murder. It seems as if Danny recollected his conversation with you about putting out the hit on Miguel and Buck for you," Evans said.

"Evidently, he is willing to testify in court about that, and if it sticks, you will never see the light of day ever again," Buck said, continuing. "From the looks of it, you don't have a leg to stand on in this case; by the way, pardon the pun."

Frankie closed his eyes and yelled for the guard to come get him and take him back to his cell. As he was being pushed back to the door, Evans yelled out, "We'll be seeing you in court soon; until then, have a nice day."

Once Frankie was alone in his cell, he looked around and sat there, realizing that he was never going to get out of this prison and that no one could help him now. He just sat there, not saying a word, looking at the walls in his cell. Frankie was thinking that if he could kill himself it would be better than living as a cripple for the rest of his life in prison and looking around his cell, he realized he couldn't even do that.

Buck and Miguel arrived back in Phoenix at nine o'clock that night. By the next morning, Buck and Rachael, with their kids, were on their way back home.

Lucas had driven down to see Amanda after getting off the flight in Phoenix and was able to spend the weekend with her, telling her all about the trip to New Jersey and all the things that had happened there. She was awestruck by the stories he told and, in her own mind, wondered how much of it was true, never questioning him, just smiling and nodding her head at what he was saying.

Smith had left a phone message for Miguel, saying that next Monday he needed to have him in the office about a new case that had popped up since he had been gone to Jersey City.

Buck and Rachael got home in the afternoon and settled down to rest for a bit before checking the phone messages on their home phone. Most of them were routine, but one stood out, saying, "Don't get too comfortable just yet; we need you to come with us on another issue."

Buck and Rachael looked at each other as they sat on the bed and closed their eyes and lay down for a nap. Whatever it was it would have to wait till tomorrow.

The End

Epilogue

Race Benton was promoted and given his own unit as lead special agent working drugs and organized crime in the New Jersey area.

Mike was put in charge as a liaison with the ATF to work arms and drug deals in the metro area of New York and New Jersey with his own team.

Joe Cagney was given an award for his part in the takedown of the Organization and promoted to work with the FBI on other organized crime families.

Claudia Smith continued working with Joe Cagney, and the two were inseparable from then on, working together on special assignments with the FBI.

Miguel was given an award for his part in the take-down of the Organization and has it proudly hanging on his wall at home, along with a medal he received from the Phoenix Police Department.

Lucas was promoted to a Field Operative for the Border Patrol and has his own team working for him in human trafficking and, when he's not busy with that, he works with Miguel and Agent Smith when needed on drug cartel issues.

Buck and Rachael went back to work as if nothing

had happened, still wondering about the message on their home phone.

Frankie never did try again to kill Miguel and his family or Buck and Rachael after that. He sat in his cell for the remainder of his life and stared at the walls.

Danny the Jackal went to prison in New Jersey and was subsequently killed by another inmate, who had sneaked into his cell in the middle of the night and murdered him while sleeping in his bed but not before he had told everything he knew to the FBI about the other organizations.

The operation of the Organization was taken over by another group who ran the drugs and human trafficking all along the East coast.